PAGAN FIRES

From the moment Arabella gazed into Seth's black eyes she was swept up into a whirlwind of passion, lust and forbidden love. Betrayed by those she had trusted, Arabella strikes out blindly in revenge: a fatal error. She is sent to the American colonies, where she is once more a victim of the pagan desires her beauty arouses in men. Haunted by memories of the one man she still loves, Arabella tries to make a new life on the plantation, but fate conspires against her . . .

LYNN GRANVILLE

PAGAN FIRES

Complete and Unabridged

LINFORD
Leicester

First published in Great Britain

First Linford Edition
published 1997

British Library CIP Data

Granville, Lynn
    Pagan fires.—Large print ed.—
Linford romance library
1. Love stories
2. Large type books
I. Title
823.9′14 [F]

ISBN 0–7089–5186–4

Published by
F. A. Thorpe (Publishing) Ltd.
Anstey, Leicestershire

Set by Words & Graphics Ltd.
Anstey, Leicestershire
Printed and bound in Great Britain by
T. J. International Ltd., Padstow, Cornwall

This book is printed on acid-free paper

eyes, which belonged to quite the most handsome man she'd ever seen. He was kneeling beside her, easing the stock of white lace at her throat.

"Apollo . . . ?" Arabella murmured. "I was flying . . . "

The man's deep laughter brought her back to reality. She sat up, wincing.

"Careful! — you've had a nasty fall."

He stood up. Arabella took his hand and was pulled to her feet. She swayed dizzily but he held her until the faintness passed. She noticed how tall and broad-shouldered he was; how white his teeth looked against the deep tan of his skin. Apollo come to earth, she thought wickedly, letting her imagination run on freely for a moment. Then her smile faded as something stirred in her memory and the years slipped back.

She was a child. It was cold and the wind was whipping into her face as she ran through the trees. She was running . . . running . . .

It was her tenth birthday. She'd risen early, slipping unnoticed into her mother's room. Lady Susan had planned a big surprise for her and she couldn't wait to find out what it was.

Her mother was lying with her face half-hidden in the bedclothes, but Arabella believed she was only pretending to be asleep. She crept towards the bed, planning to jump on her mother and tickle her. Then she saw Lady Susan's face and stopped. Something was wrong! Her mother looked so strange, her eyes wide open and staring.

"Mother . . ." she whispered, terrified. "Mother . . . ?"

Then the door opened and a maid came in. She frowned at Arabella. "You shouldn't be here."

Arabella's eyes were dark with fear. "My mother's dead, isn't she?"

"You shouldn't be here," the maid repeated. "Come back with your father when I've made her decent. Go away, child!"

Arabella backed away, shaking her head; then she turned and fled. She ran along the passage and down the main staircase on bare feet, forgetting she was in her nightgown. That wasn't her mother lying there: it was a stranger with dead, staring eyes. Dead, dead, dead . . .

The word pounded in her brain. Someone called her name as she ran through the hall, but she did not stop. At first she was not aware of the rain or the cold. She was sobbing wildly as she ran. Her mother was dead. She would never see her smile again, never hear her laughter or feel her gentle touch . . .

Her head spinning, Arabella realised she was being held tightly. Leaning her head against the man's chest, she closed her eyes as a tear ran down her cheeks; then she drew away from him.

"Thank you. It — it was just that I remembered you found me the day my mother died." She smiled up at him.

"I never did thank you for saving my life, Seth."

Seth Blackthorn shook his head. He recalled the shivering, terrified child he'd found crouching under a bush in the spinney separating his father's farm from the Pennington's park. She'd been missing for hours and was soaked to the skin when he discovered her. At first she just stared at him. He'd knelt beside her, talking to her gently until she crept into his arms. He'd never forgotten how she clung to him as he carried her home.

"I was ill. Afterwards I came to thank you, but Molly said you'd gone." Her eyes accused him. "Your mother was heartbroken when you ran away."

Seth frowned. "I wanted to find a better life than my father's."

"And did you?"

"No." He grinned ruefully. "I spent seven years at sea and I've nothing to show for it — except a few scars."

Arabella laughed, tossing her long hair so that it cascaded down her back in silken waves the colour of sunlight. Little flames of mischief danced in her sea-green eyes as she gazed into his handsome face, liking the way his curly black hair fell forward over his brow. This man was quite different from the tongue-tied youth she'd known as a child!

Molly Blackthorn had once been Lady Susan's personal maid, but she'd left to marry one of Sir William's tenants and care for her husband's young son. Despite this the two women had continued to be friends until Lady Susan's death. Arabella had often seen Seth working about the farm but he'd never taken much notice of her, except for *that* day. She could not recall what he'd said then, she only knew he had eased her pain.

Arabella became aware Seth was watching her. She felt breathless but scolded herself. She must not let her head be turned by a handsome face! Seth was the son of her father's tenant and, by his own admission, practically penniless. She sighed as the problems began to crowd in on her again.

"Are you ill?" Seth asked, seeing a flicker of pain in her eyes.

"No." Arabella smiled briefly, brushing the debris from her skirt. "I ought to be getting back — will you help me mount?"

"Of course, if you feel up to it."

Seth's voice was that of a polite stranger, hiding the storm of emotion she had aroused. He cursed himself for a fool; a moment ago they had been simply a man and a woman thrown together by fate, now she was Arabella Pennington once more and the gap between them was a chasm he could not bridge.

Arabella waited while he caught the reins and brought Firefly to her. She expected him to offer his hand, but instead he encircled her waist with both hands, lifting her effortlessly into the saddle. For a moment she looked down into his dark eyes, aware of the current of feeling between them.

"Thank you — Tell Molly I shall visit her soon."

Seth watched her ride away, a wry smile twisting his mouth.

★ ★ ★

Arabella reined in as the trees thinned and she could see the house, its red brick walls mellowed by the years to a soft rust. How she loved her home; ancient and decaying for lack of money as it was: the woods, the sweeping downs, and beyond the chalky cliffs and the sea.

Situated between the Cinque ports of Rye and Hastings, Pennington Towers was a Tudor manor house built with a fortune stolen from a Spanish galleon. It lay only a short distance from the village of Sheldrake, which formed part of the estate. To Arabella her home meant freedom. Her soul needed the peace and beauty of the Sussex countryside as much as the air she breathed.

Tomorrow Aunt Augusta and Charis

would arrive for the ball to celebrate her seventeenth birthday. It was several months late but her father had delayed because he could not afford the expense. Now, however, matters were so desperate he was gambling the estate's future on one last throw of the dice. First a lavish ball and then a season in London for his lovely daughter ... Arabella sighed. She hated the idea of being paraded by her aunt as if she were a piece of merchandise on sale to the highest bidder. But she had little choice: either she found herself a wealthy husband or stood by and watched the estate sold to pay her father's debts.

Where had all the money gone? Philip said it had been wasted over a period of many years. Sir William had lived lavishly, gambled hard and taken out a new mortgage whenever he needed funds. Not until he was on the verge of bankruptcy had he been persuaded to hand over the running of the estate to his eldest son.

Philip had tried hard but it was an almost impossible task. He'd sold the town house and most of the thoroughbred horses kept for racing at Ascot and Newmarket. Sir William's stables had been famed for their bloodstock: some of the stallions had fetched good prices, selling as far afield as Virginia, yet still it was not nearly enough.

Arabella was frowning as she went into the house. She paused at the foot of the stairs, her hand resting on the bannisters. The door of her father's study was open and she could hear angry voices; her father and Richard were quarrelling again. She wondered why her brother Richard could not be in the house more than a few hours before he and Sir William were at each other's throats. It happened every time Richard came home on leave from his regiment and the argument was always about money.

"Damn it, Richard, you can't expect father to bail you out again so soon. I warned you the last time." That was Philip's voice, milder than the other two but anxious.

Arabella knew Philip had every right to be annoyed, yet at this moment her sympathies were with Richard. She believed she understood the frustration behind his wild behaviour.

Richard was a difficult person to reach, and Arabella could only guess at the thoughts he kept so well hidden. But the bond between them had been forged in childhood when Richard appointed himself her guardian. He'd grown even more protective of her after her mother died. She longed to leap to his defence now, but knew it would be useless. Sir William could be persuaded into most things but never driven. A little smile curving the corners of her sensuous mouth, she turned towards the study.

Sir William was sitting in a high-backed chair by the fireplace, one foot propped up on a stool. He looked up as she entered, the bitter words dying on his lips.

Leaning over the back of his chair Arabella dropped a kiss on the top of his head, her eyes seeking Richard's in silent appeal.

"How are you this morning, dearest?" Arabella knelt by her father's chair. "Is your gout troubling you? Shall I ask Doctor Simmons to call on you . . . ?"

"Humph!" Sir William frowned. "Trying to sweeten me, Bella? It won't help that brother of yours; there's no money to pay his gambling debts and that's final!"

"I'm sure Richard cannot have meant to get in debt again."

"I need a loan to tide me over until next month," Richard put in quickly.

"In God's name, boy, can't you get it through your head we're on the brink of ruin?"

"And whose fault is that?"

"Insolent puppy!" A tide of hot colour swept up Sir William's neck.

Arabella flashed a warning at her brother. "He did not mean it, dearest."

She frowned at Richard. "Please apologise to father!"

Richard seemed as if he would refuse, then shrugged. "Bella is right, I shouldn't have said that — I'm sorry."

"Humph!" Sir William thumped the arm of his chair. "Don't look so worried, Bella. Philip will find the money somehow — but for the last time." His thick brows drew together. "Do you hear me, Richard?"

Richard nodded, his face white. "I won't ask you again, though how I'm expected to support myself on my pay I don't know!"

Arabella kissed her father's cheek and stood up. Tossing back her hair, she laughed. "Oh, don't look so gloomy. You know I'm going to save our fortunes by marrying a rich man. He'll have lots of lovely money, enough to pay off your wretched mortgages, Philip, and make you a generous allowance, Richard."

Philip looked anxious. "My God, I hope you manage it, Bella. If I don't come up with ten thousand pounds damn soon we shall lose most of our land, the banks are threatening to foreclose."

Arabella hid her fear, giving him a provocative glance. "Doubting me, Philip?"

Sir William laughed, thumping his chair again, "Don't be such a pessimist, Philip. Look at the girl did you ever see such a beautiful creature?"

Philip's mouth relaxed into a smile. "You're right, father, but it hardly seems fair Bella should have to bail us all out."

Arabella laughed, slipping her arm through his. "You make me sound noble. Can you really see me taking in washing for a living? I'm doing it as much for myself as the estate."

Richard had been watching her. He frowned as he noticed the stains on her gown. "What happened — did you take a tumble?"

"Yes, there's a fallen tree in the park. I didn't see it until it was too late. Firefly threw me — but I'm not hurt so there's no need to look like that!"

"Richard's thinking he'll have no chance of getting that allowance if you break your neck," Sir William muttered.

"Oh, father!" Arabella cried as she saw Richard's angry flush. "He wasn't thinking anything of the kind and you know it!"

She sighed. Her father and Richard never seemed to agree for five minutes. She knew she was Sir William's favourite and suspected it was because her mother had meant more to him than his first wife. Arabella wasn't sure what had happened; there seemed to be some mystery surrounding Richard's mother. Whatever it was it had affected Richard much more than Philip. Sir William and his eldest son tolerated each other pretty well, though there was no great affection between them.

Arabella loved all her family, but Richard was special, perhaps because he needed her. Although he was five years older, tall and well built, there was a weakness in him that was not in her or Philip.

Arabella gave her head a shake, cutting off the worrying thoughts in mid-flight. She had a great deal still to do; her aunt and cousin were arriving tomorrow and the ball was being held in three days.

She blew her father a kiss. "I must love you all and leave you — I have to check Aunt Augusta's room, you know how fussy she is . . . "

"Oh, Bella, I've invited a friend of mine down to stay for a few days. He's a keen horseman and wants to meet father — he'll arrive in time for the ball and stay on afterwards."

"Richard! You might have told me sooner." Arabella groaned as her carefully-laid plans disintegrated. "Oh well, he'll have to have the haunted room!"

Richard grinned. "I knew you wouldn't mind, Bella. Besides, he's got pots of money — at least, I think he has."

"If he's your friend I don't think he's quite what I'm looking for. I won't marry a gambler!"

Richard scowled and Arabella gurgled with laughter, escaping from the room before he could reply. She heard him follow her into the hall and call her name, but she did not turn round as she ran up the stairs and along the passage to her own room. She wasn't in the mood for a tête-à-tête with Richard. He could be so intense sometimes and she was feeling drained of energy. It had been a strain keeping up the pretence that all was well for her father's sake.

She locked the door so that no one could come in. Now that she was alone she could let her mask slip for a while. She sighed as she began to unbutton her gown; not for the world would she let her family guess what she was going through. The prospect of marrying a man simply for his fortune filled her with despair. How could she possibly bear it? And yet she must for all their sakes.

She brushed away a single tear, angry with herself for being weak, and wondering why the future looked so bleak. Of course her accidental meeting with Seth Blackthorn could have nothing to do with her mood of depression; but his handsome face had set her heart racing even before she recognised him. He'd changed so much since that day he found her in the rain, but she should have known him at once — no one else had eyes like that!

Arabella wondered if you could fall in love when you were only ten years old. She'd treasured the memory of her rescuer for the past seven years — but perhaps it was merely hero-worship. His feelings for her could have been no more than pity that day — but it was not pity in his eyes today! Today he'd made her aware of her own body, of hopes and desires she had not known existed until now. It was this which had made her run from him, knowing the gap between them was too wide. He could never enter her world, nor she his.

Arabella sighed. What an idiot she was to let herself be swayed by a handsome face and a pair of laughing eyes! She must put all her dreams aside and make up her mind to accept what the future held in store for her.

★ ★ ★

"No, Arabella, you really cannot put Lady Crawthorne next to Mr Anglesey-Jones at dinner."

"Why?" Arabella sighed. Her aunt was insisting on last-minute changes to all the arrangements for the ball and sending the housekeeper into hysterics. "Do they hate each other or something?"

Augusta Braybrooke's mouth twisted. "It is much, much worse . . . " she lowered her voice to a dramatic whisper.

"They are having an affair . . . "

"Oh . . . " Arabella fought her desire to laugh. Unfortunately for her, she happened to glance at Charis and her cousin's face was too much for her. She dissolved into giggles. "Don't be so mean, aunt, I should think they would be delighted to sit together!"

"Arabella!" Mrs Braybrooke frowned. "Foolish girl — cannot you see it would be embarrassing for them? We must appear to know nothing about the matter."

"But you do know."

"That is not the point." Augusta sighed. "If you cannot find something useful to do, you might as well go for a walk."

"May I go for a walk?" Arabella's face cleared.

Augusta looked thoughtful. "I was wondering if that woman who used to be your mother's maid — what is her name?"

"Do you mean Molly Blackthorn?"

Augusta nodded. "Do you think she

would come in tomorrow night? It's useful to have someone on hand to mend a flounce or something; none of your maids is capable. Besides, she could help Mrs Jenkins wait on the ladies."

"I suppose Molly might enjoy that, do you want me to ask her?"

"It would be a pleasant walk for you, and I'm sure she will be pleased to see you."

"Yes, it is rather a long time since I visited her." Arabella glanced at Charis who was idly turning the pages of a book. "Will you come with me?"

Before Charis could reply, her stepmother answered for her. "I don't think you should, my dear. You've had a nasty chill and the Colonel would never forgive me if you were ill again — Besides, you want to be at your best for the ball."

Charis sighed, an expression of exasperation in her brown eyes. She was small and pale with a delicate air which belied her constitution.

Sometimes her parents' fussing almost drove her wild, but she was an agreeable girl and usually gave in without making a fuss, unless the argument was really important to her.

"I'm perfectly well now, mamma," she said, giving Arabella an apologetic look. "However, I promised to help Philip with some letters; you know he detests writing letters!"

"You spoil him, Charis." Arabella laughed. "I refused point-blank."

"Yes, I know — but he's such a dear."

Charis smiled and Arabella dimpled. They were close friends and found it almost too easy to read each other's minds.

"Then I'll go alone. Is there anything you want me to do before I go, aunt?"

Augusta was studying the guest list intently. "No. Run along now, both of you, and let me get on with this."

Arabella slipped her arm through Charis', whispering: "Come on, let's escape while we can!"

Charis nodded. Outside in the hall she said, "I'll come if you really want me to, Bella."

"It doesn't matter." Arabella shrugged carelessly. "I know you would rather write Philip's letters: a labour of love, Charis?"

"Bella!" Charis flushed. "I don't know what you mean."

"No?" Arabella's brows rose. "I think you do — but poor Philip is too worried to notice at the moment."

"Is there anything I can do? Mama did say things were difficult . . . "

"That's putting it mildly; we're slowly sinking in the mire of father's debts."

"I have some money of my own . . . "

"No!" Arabella smiled at her. "You couldn't help, Charis — not without breaking the trust your maternal grandfather set up, and I'm sure your father would never allow it. Besides, we've decided I'm to marry a rich man, so it's all taken care of."

Her voice was flippant but Charis

was not deceived. "How rotten for you, Bella — but perhaps you'll meet someone really nice."

"Oh yes! He will be very tall, handsome, with bold black eyes and . . . " her voice trailed off as she realised she'd been describing Seth Blackthorn. "Don't mind me, Charis, I'm feeling sorry for myself. I think I had better go for that walk."

"I'll see you later then." Charis looked doubtful. "I'm sure it will all come right."

"Yes, of course."

Arabella made her voice light and airy, wanting to convince herself as much as Charis. The two girls parted: Charis to find Philip and Arabella to collect her shawl and parasol.

★ ★ ★

Arabella paused outside the farmhouse door, thinking Molly would be surprised to see her. It was some time since she'd visited. Her hand trembled as she knocked and her stomach fluttered at the thought of perhaps seeing Seth again.

A cheerful voice bade her enter. As she went in Molly looked up from her work, giving a cry of pleasure as she wiped her floury hands on her apron.

"If it isn't Miss Arabella," she exclaimed. "What a lovely surprise — and you with so much to do with the party and all!"

Arabella smiled. Glancing round the kitchen she felt a pang of disappointment: Seth was not here.

"Hello, Molly. I hope I'm not disturbing you?"

"You know you're always welcome. Will you sit here with me, or go through to the parlour?"

"Let me stay here with you, Molly."

Molly nodded, pleased. "I can see you're still 'my' lady's daughter; she always sat here with me, too."

Molly's eyes travelled round the large kitchen. She'd done well for herself when she married Seth's father. The boy had been a babe in arms then, accepting her as his mother. She'd been happy enough with her Tom, but it had been a source of pride to her that Lady Susan continued to visit her after her marriage, and that Arabella still came sometimes.

"My mother was always fond of you, Molly."

"As I was of her — my dear lady." Molly's eyes grew moist. "You're so like her, Miss Arabella."

"Am I?"

"Yes." Molly sniffed hard. "Will you take a glass of my pansy wine? I used the best brandy."

"No, thank you, not this morning. I really came to ask you a favour. I wondered if you would help me dress for the ball — and then you could show the ladies where to put their cloaks . . ."

Molly's eyes lit up. "Dress you for your first ball? Oh, Miss Arabella, how kind of you to think of it."

Arabella felt a pang of guilt as she

saw Molly's pleasure. "I should have asked you sooner, Molly, but I've been so busy . . . "

Molly beamed at her. "I shall come early so that I've plenty of time to dress your hair — Oh, and I'll ask Seth to fetch me afterwards. Did you know he was home?"

Arabella stood up, fussing with her shawl. "Yes, I met him by accident the other day. You must be very happy to have him back. Well, I shall look forward to seeing you tomorrow."

"Goodbye, my dear." Molly came to the door to watch her leave. "Thank you again."

Arabella turned to wave as Molly disappeared into her kitchen. The sun was high in a cloudless sky as Arabella strolled leisurely across the fields towards the spinney. It was such a lovely day with all the leaves and flowers just breaking into blossom, and she was in no hurry to be indoors again. There would be little enough time for solitary walks once she left for London with Aunt Augusta. She sighed, her eyes clouding. Would she ever be as free as this again?

"Hello."

Seth's voice startled her. She waited for him to come to her. He was carrying a gun and a sack over his shoulder, and had obviously been shooting game. Since he came from the spinney it was possible he'd been poaching on Sir William's land, but he showed no sign of embarrassment as he laid the sack at her feet.

"Hello." Arabella's heart fluttered as she gazed into his laughing eyes.

Seth grinned. "I've been poaching your father's rabbits; Molly makes a marvellous pie."

"It's as well for you we can't afford a gamekeeper these days."

Seth's brows rose. "Next you'll be telling me you're not holding a grand ball tomorrow!"

Arabella flushed as she heard the harsh note in his voice. "My father's last gamble. Tomorrow is merely a way of showing off his one remaining asset."

Seth frowned. "But it's your coming-out ball — you mean you're his asset?"

"Yes." Her voice dropped to a whisper. "I'm up for sale to the highest bidder . . . "

Seth stared in disbelief; then, as they gazed into each other's eyes, his expression softened. Wordlessly, he drew her into his arms. Arabella lifted her face to his, trembling as she waited for the inevitable. She wanted him to kiss her, but was not prepared for the violence of her feelings as she felt the touch of his lips on hers. His kiss was meant to be tender, but as he sensed her response, it changed into a demanding, passionate embrace which left them both shaken.

Arabella drew away, her eyes wide. She touched her lips with trembling fingers, aware she was no longer the innocent girl who had left home earlier this morning. Then her head had been filled with vague dreams of a romantic ideal, now she knew exactly what she wanted!

"I love you," Seth said. "I think I've loved you since you were no higher than my knee." His mouth twisted wryly. "I went away to make my fortune so that I could come back and marry the princess in the tower. What a fool I was!"

Arabella blinked away her tears. "Don't say it," she begged. "You know they would never let us marry. Besides, I have to marry a rich man, Seth. I have to!"

"How much do you need? I'll get the money somehow, Bella. I swear it!"

Arabella gave him a watery smile. "You don't understand; Philip needs ten thousand pounds urgently or the estate will be sold."

Seth's eyes hardened and his mouth set in grim determination. "I'll get it."

"How?"

Arabella was confused: this whole conversation was ridiculous. They could never marry even if Seth managed to find the money. He must know it as well as she; like her he was dreaming.

"There are ways — even for men like me," he said and his voice was sharp with bitterness as if he resented the gap between them. "Look — I'll show you. Hold out your hands." He took something from his coat.

Arabella opened her hands wide, watching as the gold coins poured through her fingers spilling on to the ground. She laughed excitedly, her eyes dancing as she dropped to her knees and scooped them up. Then she looked at him in wonder.

"Where did you get this? You told me you had nothing to show for your years at sea. There must be three hundred pounds here."

"Five." Seth grinned as he restored the coins to his pouch. "And more where that came from."

Arabella got to her feet, gazing into his black eyes. "You've been out with the gentlemen; you could only have earned this kind of money smuggling."

Seth shrugged his powerful shoulders. "Maybe — maybe not."

"You'll hang if they catch you."

"Perhaps — if I'm caught."

Arabella stared. "Aren't you even a bit scared?"

"Should I be? Are you going to report me to the Revenue of Officers, Bella?"

She shook her head, eyes sparking with mischief. "No — but it must be dangerous. Last year they shot two of the gentlemen and hung another."

Seth grinned as she revealed her knowledge of the smuggling fraternity. The gentlemen were spoken of in hushed whispers hereabouts, the silent witness of their passing holding their tongues for fear of reprisals.

His eyes gleamed as the dream he'd cherished hovered tantalisingly close. He wasn't sure when he'd begun to love Arabella; it might have been the day she crept into his arms like a wounded fawn or when he first saw her two days ago. It hardly mattered;

she'd always been there in his mind. He realised he'd been waiting all his life for this moment.

"Well," he said, his voice harsh, "is it a bargain?"

Arabella looked at him uncertainly. "You make it sound as though you're buying me."

"I thought that was the idea."

She flushed. "It isn't polite to put it so plainly. Oh, all right, I know it amounts to the same thing, but ladies are not supposed to understand . . . " her voice trailed off as he laughed.

"Can you see Sir William giving me his blessing? We would have to go away somewhere it wouldn't matter that you're a lady and I'm the son of your father's tenant. The world is a wide place, Bella; we could be happy away from all this."

"Could we?"

Arabella was suddenly doubtful as she looked at his hard face. When he kissed her she had been ready to abandon her world for him, but now she wasn't sure. Were the wild emotions he roused in her really love? Was she brave enough to leave her home and family for him, did she love him that much?

"You'll have to give me time, Seth."

His face hardened. "You mean you might accept if nothing better turns up?"

Arabella flushed. "You're cruel. I thought you loved me."

The anger drained out of him as he saw the hurt in her eyes. "I do love you — too much. I know I have no right to ask you to marry me, maybe that's why I lashed out at you."

"Oh, Seth, I do love you — but you're asking so much of me. I'm frightened. Can you understand that?"

"Yes." He sighed. "It was madness even to hope — Goodbye, Arabella."

"Seth — Seth don't go!" she cried as he picked up his gun and began to walk away.

He turned back. The gun fell to the ground as he swung her into his arms, his fingers biting deep into her flesh. He gazed down into her eyes for a long moment. Then his lips ground against hers in a kiss of fierce possession as he held her imprisoned, dominating her by the force of his willpower, draining her of all emotion except desire for him. She arched herself against his body, melting as the longing to be one with him made her weak. When he let her go she almost fell.

"Think of that, Arabella," he said. "When you're deciding who can give you what you want — what you really want. I'll be around if you decide it's me."

Arabella couldn't speak. She watched as he picked up his gun again. Then she gave a cry and ran off into the woods, leaving her parasol lying on the ground.

Seth picked it up, torn between going after her and his anger. He'd been a fool to believe even for a moment that she might care enough to leave everything and go away with him. Why should she? He wasn't the only man who would want her: she was beautiful. Even if he could get the money she so desperately needed it was nothing. Some wealthy aristocrat would give her everything she desired; he couldn't hope to compete. The gap between them was as wide as ever, all he'd done was make a fool of himself. He'd never meant her to know how he felt, but the temptation to hold her in his arms had been too strong.

Suddenly Seth laughed. He was crying for the moon! He made up his mind to forget her. There was a pretty little wench in the village who had been making eyes at him ever since he got back. Maybe tonight he would pay her a visit . . .

★ ★ ★

Arabella ran most of the way home, slowing down only when she was certain Seth wasn't following her. Part of her wanted him to come after her but commonsense told her what an idiot she was. Already she was regretting the stormy interlude in the woods; she must have been out of her mind! But when he held her in his arms nothing seemed to matter but the delicious tingling sensation seeping through her body; the desire to cling to him for the rest of her life. That was madness! How could she give up all she loved just for the pleasure of being in his arms? That kind of love was a fever in the blood, it couldn't last. What she needed was a man like her father, someone who would treat her with respect. The suspicion that such a relationship might prove boring was ruthlessly crushed. Seth was too dangerous. He would want to own her, body and soul.

She was about to rush up the stairs when Charis came into the hall and called to her. "Where have you been? Mama is annoyed with you for taking so long."

"I stayed talking to Molly. What's so terrible about that?"

"Why, nothing . . . " Charis faltered. "Oh, Bella, you've got mud on your dress . . . "

Arabella frowned. Why must Charis notice everything? "I came through the spinney and I stumbled, that's all."

"Bella — is that you?"

Arabella turned at the sound of Richard's voice. He came into the hall, followed by a tall, rather good-looking stranger.

"Richard, I did not know we had guests."

Richard's eyes went over her almost hungrily. "Only one guest — this is Christopher Allingham. Remember I told you he wanted to talk horses with the old man?"

"Oh yes." Arabella flushed. "I'm sorry I wasn't here when you arrived, Mr Allingham. I didn't expect you until tomorrow."

Arabella knew her greeting sounded ungracious, but she found Allingham's mocking stare disturbing. His cool eyes swept over her, absorbing every detail of her appearance. She was painfully conscious of the mud and leaves clinging to her skirts. Damn the man, she thought, what right had he to stand there looking so elegant when she must look a mess?

She assumed a haughty manner. "Please excuse my appearance, I have just suffered a shock." She turned to her brother. "Richard, I think there have been poachers in the woods again. Someone fired a shot and I saw a wounded bird."

"No wonder you fell, you must have been terrified," Charis cried.

"I was a little." Arabella thought she detected a gleam of disbelief in Allingham's eyes. "In fact, I'm feeling unwell. I think I shall lie down for a while."

"Damn it! He might have killed you. Did you get a look at him, Bella?" Richard frowned.

Arabella suddenly remembered the sack full of rabbits Seth had been carrying. What on earth had made her mention poaching?

"Yes. I — I caught a glimpse of him through the trees. He had red hair — and a beard I think." Arabella felt pleased with herself until she saw the expression on Allingham's face. He didn't believe her!

"I wonder if it's worth trying to find him?" Richard said.

"I shouldn't bother. He must know I saw him; he'll be long gone by now."

"I'm sure Miss Pennington is right." Allingham came to her rescue unexpectedly. "The rascal will have gone; he was possibly more startled than your sister."

Arabella blushed, knowing he was laughing at her. But he could not know of her meeting with Seth. She touched her lips, still feeling the sting of his kisses.

"I must go and change," Arabella said. "I hope to see you later, Mr Allingham."

"Of course you will," Richard said. "I told you he wants to talk horses with the old man: that should please him."

Arabella smiled, nodding distantly to Allingham. Then, she walked upstairs, holding her back very straight.

Once inside her own room she kicked off her shoes with a scream of annoyance. She was used to being taken at face value by her family. Even Aunt Augusta would never suspect her of telling an outright lie, so why should Mr Allingham? Unless he'd chosen to ride up from the village through the fields . . .

She imagined what he might be thinking if he'd seen her with Seth. Her hair was ruffled and her gown was crushed; he would think she'd been keeping a lover's tryst. Her cheeks burned as she realised how close it had been to being just that.

Arabella's heart told her she was in love with Seth, but she was the daughter of a baronet: a lady. How could she even consider stepping out of her world to marry a man so far beneath her?

It was all Christopher Allingham's fault! Arabella decided to focus her anger on him. How dare he look at her that way, as if he found her vaguely amusing! The man was infuriating. Had he seen her with Seth, would he tell Richard?

She wrenched at the tiny pearl buttons fastening her gown, tearing the silk in her impatience. She hurled the gown to the floor, then sat down at her dressing table to drag a silver-backed brush through her hair.

Damn him! Damn her father's debts! Damn everything!

The hairbrush suffered a similar fate to her gown.

Arabella grabbed a handful of her long hair, twisting it high on her head. She didn't care if he'd seen her or not. Mr Allingham was after all only a man; he shouldn't be that hard to manage. Before he left Pennington Towers he would be a little less cool, Arabella would see to that!

2

THAT night Arabella played the gracious hostess, surprising both herself and Aunt Augusta. Once Arabella noticed a gleam of appreciation in her aunt's eyes and nearly ruined everything by giggling, but seeing Allingham watching her she recovered in time.

After the company had dispensed with a dinner of green goose, venison and several roast ducks, the ladies retired to the drawing-room, leaving the gentlemen to their port. However, they were not long in following and Arabella soon found herself seated on the sofa with Richard lounging beside her and Allingham a few feet away.

Charis was at the piano-forte; Philip beside her, turning the sheets of music. Sir William and his sister had become engrossed in a game of picquet and were quarrelling noisily.

Arabella gave Christopher a cool smile. "You will find us countrified, Mr Allingham. Perhaps you and Richard would prefer to find your own diversions?"

"Not at all, Miss Pennington. I feel myself quite at home here — and your cousin plays delightfully."

"Yes, Charis has some talent I believe."

"Do you play, Miss Pennington?"

"Oh, Bella has no ear for music," Richard drawled. "She was too lazy to learn, but she can ride and shoot better than either Philip or I."

Arabella's eyes shot darts at him. "Richard! Mr Allingham will think I have no female accomplishments. My taste is for art rather than music, sir, though I enjoy listening to good music."

Allingham inclined his head. "I have no musical talent either. Like you I prefer to listen."

Arabella was silent as she searched

for a suitably cutting remark.

"Chris plans to buy land in Virginia and raise horses," Richard said. "I've thought of resigning my commission and joining him."

"Oh no!" Arabella exclaimed. "It wouldn't suit you."

Richard laughed. "Would you miss me — or do you mean I'm too lazy to make a go of it? You're probably right, though I can't see much future here — unless I can find a rich wife . . . " He glanced towards Charis and frowned; then he got up and walked over to the fireplace, watching the two at the piano-forte.

Arabella followed his glance, feeling shocked. Charis was like a sister to her: Richard couldn't be thinking of marrying her for her money! She smiled suddenly. Charis might look docile but she had a mind of her own.

Turning back to Mr Allingham, she asked: "Are you really going to Virginia?"

"Yes. There's a growing interest in

both racing and thoroughbred horses in the colonies. I think the climate of Virginia well suited to my purpose. Besides, there's room to breathe out there."

Arabella smiled. "Did you know some of father's stallions were sent to Virginia?"

"Yes, Richard told me. It was a pity your father had to sell — still, his loss was Virginia's gain."

"It almost broke father's heart, but his health would not allow him to continue racing so there was no point in maintaining the stables."

"Quite." Allingham studied his hand. "This house must be very old, Miss Pennington."

"Yes. It was built by the first Pennington after he'd snatched his fortune from a Spanish galleon. He was knighted by the Queen for his generous contribution to her coffers. You are in the company of thieves and rogues, sir!" Arabella couldn't resist the jibe.

"That's better. I thought you meant to freeze me to death."

"What can you mean?" Arabella asked innocently, her lips twitching.

"I would be grateful if you would show me over the house, Miss Pennington. My home was quite modern — we have no ancestors to boast of I'm afraid."

"Really?" Arabella's eyes swept over him. She stood up. "Come, I will show you the picture gallery."

Christopher offered his arm and they left together. In the hall she paused, looking thoughtful. "This part of the house was extensively renovated by my grandfather, however, the east wing has been left virtually untouched."

"Then that is what I should like to see."

"We shall need some light — will you bring one of the candelabra?"

He picked up a branch of candles and followed her obediently.

"The library was converted in my great-grandfather's time — the screen you see there was carved by Grinling Gibbons."

"I thought as much: it is very fine."

They passed into the next room.

"The ceiling in here was painted in about 1690 by an Italian who worked in many of the great houses of the time. This room was used by the Duke of Monmouth when he stayed here shortly before the uprising. John Pennington chose the wrong side and was disgraced when Monmouth was hanged; but he managed to crawl back into favour with William of Orange."

"You make an excellent guide." Allingham's lips twitched.

"This is the portrait gallery; the panelling and ceiling are original." She stopped in front of a large, dark painting. "This was Sir Ralph — the pirate."

"A privateer surely!"

Arabella raised her brows. "Is there a difference?"

He laughed. "Not if you were a Spaniard. You constantly surprise me.

You are not afraid of the truth, and yet you are not always so honest."

"Oh?" Arabella's heart pounded. He had seen her with Seth!

They moved on down the gallery until they reached the portrait of Arabella's mother. "You have no need to tell me who this is . . . " He looked at Arabella. "She was lovely — but not as beautiful as her daughter."

Arabella flushed. "You flatter me, sir."

"I'm sure you know you are an exceptionally lovely woman. I cannot be the first to tell you so."

"What makes you think that?"

Allingham raised his brows. "I believe you understand me. I will not embarrass you by speaking more plainly."

Arabella couldn't look at him. "You saw me with . . . it wasn't what you thought . . . "

He laughed. "Don't be alarmed, I have no intention of betraying your secret."

Arabella drew a sharp breath as she

saw the look in his eyes. The ice had suddenly melted. Her cheeks burned and she moved quickly to the next portrait.

"Don't you think this is very like Richard? Father wants to have my likeness taken but I find it too boring to sit still for hours on end."

She heard his soft laughter and felt the touch of his hands on her neck, shivering as he caressed her. "Don't! — please."

"Is that the prerogative of the young man I saw you with? He's not worthy of you. A woman as lovely as you should look higher."

"At a man of the world — like yourself perhaps?"

"Perhaps."

Arabella turned away. "I think we should join the others."

"If you wish." His mouth curved in a mocking sneer.

Arabella suddenly wished she had not set out to arouse his interest in her. What had begun as a game had become a duel of wits, and she was a little afraid of him.

* * *

Molly piled Arabella's hair up on top of her head, allowing one long ringlet to fall on her neck, then stood back to admire her work.

"You look beautiful," she said. "My lady would've been so proud of you."

Arabella twisted and turned before the mirror, admiring her gown of white satin, encrusted with tiny pearls and wreathed with silver gauze. Giving a cry of delight, she turned to Molly.

"You've made me look beautiful!"

Molly shook her head. "You are beautiful. You'll set some hearts fluttering tonight."

"Shall I?"

Arabella's laughter had a brittle edge. She was close to tears as she realised Seth would not be there to see her in all her finery.

The door opened and Charis came

in. "Are you ready, Bella? Oh, you do look lovely!"

The interruption was timely. Arabella's chin went up as she picked up her fan. She had a duty to her family: she must remember she was a Pennington.

"Yes, I'm ready — Shall we go down?"

The two girls joined Mrs Braybrooke as she welcomed the stream of guests. She kept them with her for nearly an hour and Arabella's smile was becoming fixed by the time she was released. But at last she and Charis were allowed to join the other young people in the ballroom, and were immediately besieged by eager gentlemen. Within minutes Arabella's card was full.

"I hope you saved a dance for me?"

Arabella looked into the hard eyes. Allingham's manner was so cold she wondered if she'd imagined that interlude in the gallery. She studied her card, thankful it was full.

"I'm sorry — I'm afraid you're too late."

"May I see?" He took the card from her, striking out the name of the man who had engaged her for the supper dance, replacing it with his own.

"You can't do that! Mr Barlow is the son of one of my father's oldest friends."

"Then point him out to me please."

Arabella stared. Despite herself she was intrigued. She indicated a fair-haired gentleman, just now dancing with Charis. "But what will you say to him?"

Allingham smiled. "I shall endeavour to persuade him that my need is greater — but I see your partner coming. I shall return later."

Arabella turned to greet her partner as Allingham walked away, dismissing the incident. Robert Barlow was not wealthy enough to be considered as a suitor, but she knew he believed himself a little in love with her and doubted he would yield to Allingham.

As the evening passed, Arabella found she was enjoying herself. It was years since a ball like this had been held at Pennington Towers, but her father had managed to keep up the tradition of a Christmas party and so most of the guests were old friends — with some exceptions. Brothers, nephews and cousins had been summoned home from Oxford and Cambridge specially for the occasion.

The evening was made easier for Arabella by the absence of any likely suitors. Of all the gentlemen presented to her only one had a sizeable fortune, and he was engaged. However, the ball was merely a prelude to her season in London. It would ensure that she and Charis received plenty of invitations — and it was less expensive than holding a ball in Town!

Gradually Arabella forgot her heartache. It was hard to resist the compliments showered on her by her partners. She danced, laughed and sipped her champagne, pretending that everything was just as it should be. Her father was the wealthy Sir

William Pennington and she was his spoilt daughter without a care in the world . . .

Arabella found herself momentarily alone. The last dance before supper had begun and Robert was nowhere in sight. Angry at his desertion, she turned to leave the ballroom before Allingham could claim her. She was too late.

"My dance I believe, Miss Pennington."

Arabella glared at him. "I must beg you to forgive me — I'm feeling a little warm. If you will excuse me, I shall go out on to the terrace."

Allingham seemed unmoved. "Pray allow me to escort you."

"I prefer to go alone," Arabella hissed.

"Forgive me, but I insist on accompanying you. You are obviously unwell."

Arabella gave him a murderous look but accepted his arm, letting him lead her from the ballroom. They were not alone for several other couples could be seen walking along the terraces.

"These gardens are beautiful," Allingham said. "Tomorrow I hope to walk as far as the lake and that delightful pseudo ionic temple. I presume the landscaping was the work of Capability Brown?"

"Yes. My grandfather spent a fortune importing rare plants from China, Japan — even the New World."

Allingham nodded. "Richard tells me my room is supposed to be haunted, but I've seen no sign of a ghost."

Arabella sighed. "It used to be our governess's room. There's a secret passage leading from it to m . . . to another bedroom. Richard and I discovered it. We used it to play tricks on the governess. She believed it was haunted."

Allingham looked thoughtful. "I wonder why Richard was so secretive about it. He refused to explain."

"I really have no idea." She shivered as she saw he was watching her with the alertness of a hunter stalking its prey. "I think we should go into supper now."

"As you please."

Arabella turned to leave and found herself suddenly caught in his arms. She glanced round, discovering that everyone else had disappeared.

"Please — let me go."

Allingham glanced down, smiling coldly. "In a moment. You have no need to fear me. I find you fascinating." His fingers traced the arch of her white throat. "Few women interest me as you do, Arabella. I cannot help wondering what lies beneath the veneer of that lovely face."

Arabella looked at him uncertainly. "Are you asking me to marry you?"

Allingham laughed. "It might even be worth it."

Arabella made a determined effort to free herself, feeling surprised when he let her go. He smiled as he saw disbelief in her eyes.

"Were you expecting me to force you? Oh no, I want your willing surrender — nothing less would appeal to me."

"Then you will be disappointed, Mr Allingham. Now I am going into supper."

The mocking look was back in his eyes as he stood aside to let her pass, but he made no attempt to follow her.

As Arabella entered the supper room, she saw Robert Barlow standing alone. She went up to him, a militant sparkle in her eyes. "How dare you let that man cheat you out of your dance?"

"You mean you don't have an understanding with him?" His face fell. "I'm sorry, Bella, but he hinted you were in love with him."

"I detest him!"

Robert looked more cheerful. "Good. I don't like the fellow either. Can I get you some supper — just to show you've forgiven me?"

"I'll have a little chicken and some of the asparagus in aspic." She bestowed a brilliant smile on him as she saw

Allingham come in.

She was conscious of him watching her throughout supper, but when she returned to the ballroom he had disappeared. The remainder of the evening passed without incident. Arabella danced every dance, leaving the ballroom only when the musicians had at last stopped playing.

"Wasn't it a lovely party?" Charis asked as they prepared to go upstairs.

"Yes." Arabella hesitated at the foot of the stairs. "Charis, you go up. I want to thank the servants for making the ball such a success."

Charis looked surprised. "Couldn't you ask Mrs Jenkins to do that in the morning?"

"I could — but don't you realise how much work a party like this makes for them? The least I can do is to say thank you."

"I suppose so. Goodnight then." Charis watched as she walked away. Arabella was behaving very oddly lately!

Arabella's heart was racing as she made her way to the kitchens. She could not hide the truth from herself: she knew she was paying a visit below stairs in the hope of seeing Seth. If he had come to fetch Molly he would wait for her in the large kitchen where the servants took their meals.

Arabella paused on the stairs as the sound of music reached her: someone was playing a fiddle. The music was wild, hauntingly-sad and unlike anything she'd ever heard. On the threshold of the servants' hall, she stopped and stared in amazement.

A man and a woman were moving in time with the music, their bodies swaying sensuously as they circled each other. The woman provocative, inviting; the man demanding as he bent her back over his arm, his lips inches from hers. They seemed to be performing some pagan ceremony of love and the sight sent a shaft of pain through Arabella. The girl was one of the maids — but the man was Seth!

The plaintive music died abruptly and the dancers stood still, suspended like clockwork figures that had wound down. Arabella realised everyone was looking at her, waiting for her to speak. She felt like an intruder and raised her head proudly. No one must guess that inside she was seething with jealousy and pain.

"I came to thank you all. I wanted you to know how much I appreciate your hard work these past few days . . ."

There was silence, then Mrs Jenkins came towards her. "You surprised us, Miss Arabella. We all believed you would be worn out and on your way to bed. It was thoughtful of you to come . . ."

But unwelcome, Arabella thought, realising her mistake. The servants did not want her in their world: she did not belong.

"I must go — Molly will be waiting."

Arabella glanced at Seth, accusation in her eyes. "I shall not keep her long. Goodnight, everyone."

"Goodnight, miss." A chorus of voices.

Arabella's dignity carried her as far as the stairs; then she began to hurry, lifting her full skirts in her haste to escape.

"Arabella — wait!"

Arabella glanced over her shoulder, redoubling her efforts as she saw Seth at the foot of the stairs. The tears were very close as she fled through the dining room, darting into her father's study in desperation as she heard Seth following. She covered her face with her hands, sobbing bitterly. Then the door opened and Seth came in, his tall figure outlined in the light of a grey dawn. He closed the door.

Arabella jumped up, prepared for flight. "Please — leave me alone."

"Why are you crying?"

"I'm not." Arabella choked, brushing away her tears.

"Liar," he said, his voice soft. "I was teaching Rose a gipsy dance: she means nothing to me. I love you, Arabella."

"Oh, Seth — it's so hopeless." Arabella laid her head against his chest as he drew her close.

"Not if you love me enough."

Arabella looked up at him. "I do love you but . . . "

His mouth silenced her with a kiss which banished all rational thought. She threw her arms around his neck, clinging to him desperately, her whole body throbbing with love. She was trembling when he released her, aware that nothing really mattered to her but this feeling between them.

"Oh, Seth . . . " she breathed. "Love me — love me now. I want to belong to you."

Seth's mouth twisted wryly. "Don't tempt me, my darling, you don't know what you're saying."

"I do. I do!"

He sighed. "I can't risk it. If I'm to get the money you want I must leave for France immediately — it may be some months before I can arrange a cargo. Ten thousand pounds is a lot of money."

"Oh Seth . . . " Arabella sobbed. "Smuggling is so dangerous: you could be killed."

Seth laughed. "The Devil looks after his own. I made you a promise, and I mean to keep it. Besides, if you let your family face ruin you might never forgive yourself — or me."

"You are risking your life for me."

"I want you more than I've ever wanted anything in my life."

"Then love me now."

Seth groaned. "You are a witch, Bella. I may never say no to you again in my life — but God knows what would happen if you were to have a child! I won't risk it; for your sake."

"Then just hold me for a moment." Arabella trembled as he took her in his arms. "I'm so afraid, Seth."

"Don't be, my love." He stroked her

hair. "I'm going to leave you now. Wait before you follow me; in case anyone is still about."

"When shall I see you again?"

"As soon as I can arrange it. Wait for me, Bella."

"I will — oh, I will."

"Remember I love you and I won't fail you."

"Seth, kiss me again."

"Witch!" He brushed her lips with his own, leaving quickly before his desire sapped his willpower.

After he'd gone Arabella sat down, fighting to regain her composure. If her father or brothers guessed she'd met Seth like this they would forbid her to see him again. Sir William was an indulgent parent but he would never allow her to marry Seth even if he succeeded in getting the money they needed . . .

Hearing a slight noise, Arabella turned to see a figure emerge from the shadows at the far end of the room.

"I presume Sir Galahad has left us?" Allingham's voice made her shudder. "What a fool the man must be to refuse your charming offer."

Arabella stared at him. "You heard . . . "

"I found it most interesting. Smuggling, seducing a young woman of good family — I wonder what Sir William would do if he knew . . . "

Arabella knew exactly what her father would do: Seth's parents would lose the farm and Seth would be arrested for smuggling.

She drew a deep breath. "What do you want?"

"But you know what I want."

"No!" Arabella gasped, her face white.

Allingham shrugged. "It is obviously my duty to protect you from yourself unless — unless you could find a way of persuading me . . . "

Arabella closed her eyes, feeling sick. "I must have time to think."

"But of course. You are tired, my

dear. We shall talk again when you are rested. I believe you will see things more clearly then."

Arabella opened her eyes, anger flaring. "You disgust me. I hate you!" she cried. Then, whirling round, she wrenched the door open and fled.

* * *

Arabella slept little that night. The thoughts went round and round in her head, reducing her to despair. What was she to do? She no longer doubted her love for Seth. Why hadn't she gone with him last night? Philip must find another way of saving the estate. Suddenly Arabella jumped out of bed. She would go to Seth now; they could leave for France together.

Dressing quickly, she hurried down to the stables. Her groom was surprised to see her so early but quickly saddled her mare. Arabella felt a sense of release as she rode — at last she'd had the courage to take what she wanted from life.

Molly was in the yard when Arabella arrived. She looked at her in astonishment. "My goodness, you're up early." Then, as she saw Arabella's tense expression. "Is something wrong?"

Arabella flushed. "I have a message for Seth — is he here?"

Molly shook her head. "I suppose it's about those fallen trees. Seth must've forgotten he promised to clear them. He left early this morning."

"No!"

Arabella's agonised cry startled Molly. "Are you sure nothing is wrong?"

"No, I'm fine." Arabella's voice was tense. "I must go now." She turned her horse and began to canter across the fields. Wild thoughts of following Seth to France chased through her head. There must be some way she could trace him. If she could find a ship — No, it was useless, she had no idea where to look for him. She must stay and face it out. Allingham couldn't have meant what he'd said last night. He must have been drunk.

★ ★ ★

By staying close to her cousin all day Arabella managed to avoid being cornered by Christopher, but he waylaid her that evening when she came down, forcing her to enter the library with him.

"Please allow me to join the others — they will be waiting dinner for us."

"Certainly — when I have your answer."

Arabella bit her lip. "You cannot mean what you said last night — you would not force me to . . . "

"No, not force, my dear. You shall come to me of your own free will."

"I shall never do that."

Allingham shrugged. "Then you leave me no alternative."

Arabella looked at him pleadingly. "Please don't make me — please . . . "

"The choice is yours. I know the

secret passage leads from your bedroom to mine; I discovered it this afternoon. No one need ever know of our — little arrangement."

"You are evil — cruel!"

"Possibly. Shall we join the others now?"

Arabella nodded, her face pale as he opened the door. He offered her his arm, looking amused as she refused and swept on ahead of him.

They joined the others in the annexe where everyone had gathered for a drink before dinner. Arabella went to sit next to her father, forcing herself to smile as he teased her about the ball.

"What do you think of my girl?" He glanced at Allingham from beneath hooded lids. "She'll take London by storm, eh?"

"Miss Pennington is one of the most beautiful girls I've ever seen," Allingham replied smoothly.

Arabella flushed as she met the challenge of his eyes. For a moment she was tempted to confess everything to her father, but as she saw his face beaming with pride, she knew she could not. In that moment she admitted Allingham had won. She closed her eyes, holding back the tears. The thought of him kissing her . . . touching her . . . filled her with horror. But what else could she do?

The butler announced dinner and Arabella went into the dining room, Sir William leaning heavily on her arm. She noticed he was looking tired tonight and her heart contracted with pain. Why must her happiness depend on betraying her father's trust?

"Something wrong, Bella?"

She shook her head. "No — I'm just tired I expect."

"Nonsense! A young girl like you should be able to manage a dozen balls!"

Arabella laughed but did not reply. She took her place at the dinner table, sipping her wine. She drained her glass, allowing it to be refilled. The wine warmed her, steadying her as she felt

Allingham's eyes on her.

Suddenly anger and pride flowed through her. He had won but she would not let him make her crawl. If she had to pay the price for his silence, then she would do it boldly, with style. She lifted her glass to him in a salute.

★ ★ ★

Arabella looked at her reflection. Her long hair was loose on her shoulders, shimmering like a golden cloud in the candle-glow. Her face was pale but her eyes glittered with pride. She'd drunk more wine than usual tonight but not enough to make her intoxicated. Her mind was quite clear as she pressed the knot in the carved panel behind her bed, watching as part of the wainscot slid back to reveal a dark passage. She picked up her candle and stepped in.

She walked slowly, her nightgown trailing on the dusty floor, remembering the games she and Richard had played here as children, deliberately shutting her mind to the reason for her journey tonight. At the end of the passage she hesitated, her courage almost failing. She couldn't. She couldn't! But if she did not Molly might have to leave her home, and Seth would be arrested, perhaps killed. Arabella knew she would do anything rather than let that happen.

Allingham was sitting by the fireplace when the panel slid back. He stood up as he saw her, a gleam of triumph in his eyes.

"I knew you would come."

Arabella stepped into his bedroom. "I had no choice," she replied, her eyes scornful.

Allingham smiled. "You have courage, my dear, perhaps that's why I admire you. I might even have married you if I did not need Julia's money so badly."

"Julia?" Arabella felt as if she were suffocating.

"My fianceé — but we shall not speak of her."

Allingham moved towards her. "I've never seen such a beautiful creature."

"Let me go — please let me go," Arabella cried, her nerve wavering as he touched her hair.

"Beautiful — your skin is perfection, like satin . . . "

Arabella shivered as he untied the strings of her nightgown, easing it down over her shoulders so that it slithered to the ground. His eyes seemed to devour her as she stood proudly before him, lingering on her high, firm breasts and her smooth, flat belly. She wanted to cover herself but she could not move.

She waited as if in some terrifying nightmare as he slipped off his black satin robe and stood before her naked, watching her face. He laughed softly, drawing her against him so that she could feel the scorching heat of his skin and the throbbing urgency of his need. Arabella remained absolutely still as he kissed her neck, then her breasts, running his tongue between them with little darting movements. She gasped as she felt a stirring of desire deep within her. She couldn't want this!

Christopher laughed as he bent down and gathered her up in his arms, carrying her to the bed. Lying back against the pillows, she stared up at him, her eyes wide. He bent over her, catching the rosy nipples between his teeth and gently nibbling.

Arabella drew a shuddering breath as his hands caressed her. She hated him and what he was doing to her, but her body could not resist the sensuous persuasion of his touch. She was on fire, her pulses throbbing with a shameful urgency. His flesh burned her thighs; she felt his hands parting her legs and the hardness of his maleness pressing against her, insistent, ruthless. Then, just as he was about to enter her, she cried out and tried to push him away; but he only laughed, thrusting into her savagely.

Arabella screamed with pain. He looked surprised, as though he had not expected it; but the steady rhythm of his thrusting did not falter and gradually the pain was forgotten as she found herself swept up in a mounting fever. She writhed beneath him, her cries becoming frenzied as she lost control. He hushed her with a kiss as he spilled himself inside her.

Arabella moaned softly as the spasms shook her body. Then, exhausted, she turned her face to the pillow, tears of shame sliding down her cheeks. She felt humiliated as she thought of his triumph at her surrender.

"I'm sorry I hurt you. I did not realise you were still a virgin."

Arabella opened her eyes. "What do you mean?"

"I would have been more gentle with you if I'd known I was the first."

Arabella sat up, her eyes flashing angrily. "I suppose you thought I was a whore!"

He shook his head, getting up to slip on his robe. "No — I simply meant you are the kind of woman most men want to make love to. I'm glad I was the first — but there will always be some man for you."

"No. I shall love only one man as long as I live."

He smiled his disbelief. "You couldn't be that stupid, my dear. You're far too intelligent and beautiful to waste your talents on an ignorant peasant. You should marry an old man for his money — then you can take your pick of lovers. Women like you have ruled empires throughout history . . . "

Arabella's cheeks burned as she heard the cynical note in his voice. "You beast. I hate you!"

Christopher laughed. "You're even lovelier when you're angry."

Arabella snatched up her nightgown, but before she could reach the entrance to the secret passage, he had caught her. She sank her teeth into his hand and he hit her.

"Brute! You've had what you wanted, now let me alone."

"Oh no, my sweet vixen, I haven't had near enough of you yet."

Arabella looked at him in horror. "You mean . . . "

"You will come to me every night while I stay here."

"You cannot make me."

"Oh, but I can — what would your father say if he knew you'd come here tonight?"

Arabella paled. "I'll tell him you raped me."

"In my room?" Allingham laughed.

Arabella stared at him. He had her just where he wanted her; she was his slave for as long as he desired her, and he wanted her again already.

"No — please," she whispered, backing away.

"Please yes," he replied mockingly. "I've got you, my hot little wench, and there's nothing you can do about it."

★ ★ ★

"So you want to live in the colonies?" Sir William eyed his guest speculatively.

"Ain't your own country good enough for you?"

Allingham laughed. "I suppose I really want the challenge of a new life in a new country. I shall always be an Englishman at heart."

"So I should think," grumbled Sir William. "Perhaps you can knock some sense into a few heads out there: they tell me the colonists talk of breaking away from the Crown . . . "

"I doubt it will come to anything as desperate as that, sir. Everyone grumbles about taxes and the colonists were within their rights to resist the Stamp Act. It was against the charters granted to them when the land was settled, as Rockingham admitted when it was repealed. Chatham should never have agreed to new forms of taxation: it was bound to lead to trouble."

"You talk a deal of sense, young man." Sir William shot a sharp glance at his daughter. "What are you looking so glum about — sorry Allingham's off tomorrow, eh?"

"Father!" Arabella's cheeks burned as she imagined his shock if he guessed the truth: but he must never know!

"It's a pity you couldn't persuade him to stay: he'd have kept you in line, girl."

Arabella saw a gleam of amusement in Christopher's eyes. She turned her head aside, seething with suppressed anger. "I think I shall go riding — if you will excuse me, father."

"Go with her, Allingham," Sir William urged. "You can try out that stallion of mine and keep an eye on this filly at the same time."

"I shall be pleased to accompany Miss Pennington if she will permit me."

Arabella swallowed hard, hiding her fury. She could hardly forbid him when Sir William had suggested it. "I need to change. I will meet you in twenty minutes, Mr Allingham."

"Such haste, Miss Pennington, it will take me at least half an hour to change."

Arabella tossed her head as she flounced out of the study. If only there were some way of wreaking her revenge on him without betraying herself! So engrossed in her own thoughts was she that she did not immediately notice the housekeeper trying to attract her attention.

"I don't like to trouble you, miss — but Rose says she'll only talk to you." Mrs Jenkins looked uncomfortable.

"Rose?" Arabella's attention was caught. Rose had been dancing with Seth on the night of her ball. "What about Rose?"

"The wretched girl has got herself in trouble — will you see her, miss?"

Arabella nodded. "Where is she?"

"In my sitting room. I told her to wait while I asked if you would speak to her."

"Very well. Wait here while I talk to her."

Mrs Jenkins looked as if she wanted to protest but was silenced by Arabella's frown.

Rose was sitting in a chair by the window, her face red and patchy as if she'd been crying. She stood up as Arabella entered.

"Is it true, Rose?" Arabella asked, pity stirring in her heart.

"Yes, miss. I'm sorry, miss."

"Will the father of your child marry you?"

Rose looked up. "He's gone, miss. I was sure he would wed me — but he's run off and left me."

Arabella stared at her. "Gone? Who was it, Rose?"

"Seth Blackthorn."

Arabella's face paled. "It couldn't be — you're lying!"

"It were him." Rose suddenly began to cry. "Will I be turned off, miss?"

Arabella resisted the temptation to slap her. Hatred and jealousy flared up in her so that she seemed to see Rose's face through a red mist. She wanted to kill her! She fought down her anguish, breathing deeply. Rose was not to blame. She had been used, as Arabella had been used. Men were hateful and vile. All of them!

"I'm afraid my father will insist you go, Rose — but I will see you are given a year's wages. Is there anywhere you can go?"

"I've an aunt in Hampshire . . . "

"You can stay until the end of the week. I'll tell Mrs Jenkins."

Rose began to snivel. "Men are rotten. He warned me but I wouldn't listen . . . "

Arabella stared at her, then turned and went out. She gave Mrs Jenkins her instructions, squashing the housekeeper's burst of outrage.

"Rose has been foolish, that's all. Please do as I say, Mrs Jenkins. Now, excuse me, I have to change."

Arabella ran up to her room, tearing off her gown in a rage. Seth was the father of Rose's child: he'd lied to her! She felt sick and for a moment the room whirled about her. He was as false as Christopher Allingham. How she detested that man; but he would not use her again, no matter what!

Pulling on her riding gown, she rushed out of the room and down the stairs. She had no intention of waiting for Allingham; She wanted to be alone, alone with this terrible pain in her heart.

Arabella rode furiously. It was colder today and the wind stung her eyes, making them run. She rubbed her hand across her face: she wasn't crying! No man was worth crying for. But it hurt, it hurt badly. Seth had lied to her . . .

Hearing the sound of galloping hooves behind her, she glanced over her shoulder and saw she was being pursued. Instinctively, she urged the mare on faster.

"Bella — for God's sake wait!"

Richard's voice reached her. Reluctantly she brought the mare to a halt, waiting for him.

"Damn it, Bella, I thought I'd never catch you! You've got to come back to the house now . . . "

Arabella stared at him, feeling a start of fear. "What is it, Richard?"

"Father — he's had some kind of an attack. Chris went for the doctor . . . "

But she was no longer listening. Richard wheeled his horse about, calling to her to wait, but she would not listen. He caught up with her as she reached the stables. She flung herself from the mare's back, stumbling over her long skirts as she ran up to the house, leaving Richard trailing behind her.

At the door of her father's study she met the elderly physician who had tended the family ills for as long as she could remember. He stared at her and she saw there were tears in his eyes.

"I'm sorry, my dear. I was too late."

"Too late?" she echoed. "You mean . . . "

She rushed past him into the study, stopping short as she saw her father lying on the sofa. Some of the servants had gathered round him but they parted as she approached.

"Father . . . " she whispered. "Oh no . . . " Her voice rose to a scream. She flung herself to her knees beside him, clasping his body in a frenzy of grief.

"Stop that!"

She was pulled off her father's body and yanked to her feet. She shook her head wildly, beating at Allingham with her fists and screaming.

He hit her hard across the face. She stopped screaming and stared at him, shocked and bewildered. Then the room whirled about her and she fainted.

★ ★ ★

Arabella came to herself lying in her own bed. The sun was streaming in at the window and it was morning. For a few seconds she could not think why her eyelids felt so stiff or why she was so utterly miserable; then it all came flooding back. She turned her face to the pillow as the tears flowed. She could hardly believe her father was dead: she had loved him so much! Memories twisted in her like a blade. Somehow she had never expected him to die: not for years!

She was wracked by dry, painful sobs. Her tears were all shed, only the grief remained and the guilt . . . Guilt because she had planned to run away with a man who did not deserve her love. Guilt for the shame she'd brought on her name by succumbing to Allingham's blackmail. How she hated him! He thought he was her master: he should learn how much she despised him!

She jumped out of bed and threw on her wrap. She would go to his room one last time: to tell him how much she detested him!

The panel slid back and she stepped through it, glancing at the empty bed. She was too late: he had gone. Then she saw a man standing in the shadows of the window hangings.

"Christopher, I'm glad I caught you . . . " she broke off as the man moved into the light and she saw his face. "Richard!"

Richard's eyes were hard as he looked at her, taking in her tousled hair and carelessly tied wrap. "I did not believe Chris — until now."

Arabella stared at him. "Christopher told you . . . " Her legs felt weak. "Where is he?"

"He left last night." Richard's voice was accusing. "I've been waiting all night. I had to know if it was true."

"Gone?" Arabella felt cheated. She was to have no chance of revenge: and he'd betrayed her to Richard! "What else did he tell you?"

"What more could there be?" Richard looked at her scornfully. "He thought I should know in case there was a child . . . God! I was so humiliated. I wanted to kill him — and you!"

Arabella's face was white. "Why don't you?"

Richard lashed out at her, leaving

a dark red mark on her pale skin. "Bitch! Were you so hot for him that you had to come now — with father lying upstairs?"

She felt the hurt twist inside her. How could Richard say that to her? "It wasn't like that. I love father . . . "

"Is that supposed to make it better?" Richard looked as if he hated her.

"Don't — I can't bear it!"

She was crying now, trembling. If she had ever needed his love it was now, but his eyes were hard and angry.

"Pull yourself together," he snarled. "And get back to your room before the servants see you!"

Arabella looked at him fearfully. "You haven't told Philip?"

Richard made a sound of disgust in his throat. "He would never believe you hadn't been forced — nor would I if Chris hadn't told me about the secret passages. No one knew of them but us — not even Philip."

Pride made her strike back. "So you despise me now. You are like all the others: hypocrites. It's all right for a man to bed as many women as he pleases but when your sister takes a lover you start mouthing morality."

Anger and frustration leapt in Richard's eyes but she did not notice. Turning to leave the way she had entered, she glanced over her shoulder.

"Don't worry about a scandal; if I am with child I shan't come to you for help."

"Bella! Come back, you little fool . . . " Richard gave a strangled cry as the panel slid to behind her. He smashed his fist against the wall, knowing he dare not follow. He was tormented with pictures of her in Allingham's arms, enmeshed in his own private hell. "Damn it, Bella," he groaned. "Oh God — why am I cursed like this?"

Back in her own room Arabella found the desire to weep had left her. She had a cold empty feeling in the pit of her stomach. Richard's bitterness had hurt her more than Christopher's betrayal. Richard was her brother; there had always been a special relationship between them. He could have listened to her story before judging her: but he hadn't. He'd raged like a jealous lover.

Arabella shook her head. No, she was imagining it. He could not be jealous; he was her brother. He was simply angry because she'd disgraced his name.

She began to brush her hair with long, rhythmic strokes, finding the action soothing. The reflection in her mirror no longer showed her the face of an uncertain girl. It was a woman who looked back at her. A beautiful woman with a wide sensuous mouth and sea-green eyes that glittered like diamonds.

3

ARABELLA looked down at the wet pavements below and sighed. It was raining too hard to think of taking a walk and she was bored. It was now five months since her father's death, and she was staying with Charis at the house of Catherine Pollard, her cousin's aunt. They had been in Bath for two days and so far it had not stopped raining.

Having taken a chill on the morning of Sir William's funeral, Arabella had been very ill for a time. Charis refused to go to London without her and so the visit was abandoned. Richard returned to his regiment, to Arabella's relief; and everyone was very kind, especially Charis who had appointed herself Arabella's champion.

For several weeks Arabella had been immersed in her grief. The sight of her father's empty chair was enough to reduce her to tears, and so she was grateful when Charis insisted on carrying her off to Bath.

Now, she turned as Charis entered.

"We have visitors," Charis said smiling. "I could hardly credit it in this weather — but they are here and Aunt Catherine would like you to come down."

"Visitors?" Arabella's spirits lifted. "I'm glad you persuaded me to come, Charis. You've been so good to me."

Charis shook her head. "It wasn't goodness. I'm very fond of you."

Arabella smiled. She wondered whether if she'd been more like Charis, Allingham would have asked her to marry him instead of seducing her; but Charis would never have met Seth in secret. Anyway, Arabella would never have married Christopher. Thank God she'd been spared the humiliation of bearing his child!

Two gentlemen were seated in Mrs Pollard's elegant drawing room. They stood up as the girls entered, looking eager.

Mrs Pollard smiled as she introduced them. "Lord Greenvale, Mr Sommerton, may I introduce my guests — my niece, Charis Braybrooke — and Miss Arabella Pennington. Miss Pennington is in mourning for her father."

There was a murmur of sympathy from the gentlemen, then one of them moved to set a chair for Arabella. She accepted it with a smile which hid her thoughts. His care for her was all a sham; did he expect her to swoon or dissolve into tears? But wasn't that what all men wanted, a delicate, fragile flower to protect? Very well then, that was what she would be!

"You are very kind," she said, sighing.

He looked pleased. "Not at all, Miss Pennington. I am sorry to hear of your father's death — had he been ill long?"

"No, it was very sudden . . . " Now the tears on her lashes were genuine.

She twisted her kerchief, wishing he would speak of something else.

"My cousin was ill for a long time," Charis said. "I persuaded her to come to Bath in the hope that she would recover her spirits in company."

"Oh yes," agreed Lord Greenvale at once. "We must all look after her and see if we can make her smile again."

He sat down beside Arabella and proceeded to make determinedly cheerful conversation. She answered him in a quiet, gentle voice, letting him draw her out slowly. He was, she thought, exactly the kind of man she'd hoped to find. Although many years her senior, he carried his years lightly and was still an attractive man: and obviously wealthy. Just the type of man Christopher had advised her to marry.

She suddenly realised he was asking her a question.

"I know you cannot attend large gatherings, Miss Pennington — but I do hope you will feel able to come to my aunt's soireé this evening?"

Arabella smiled. "I should like that — if Mrs Pollard thinks it proper for me to do so?"

Catherine nodded her approval. "The Countess is one of my oldest friends. We shall be delighted to come, sir."

Robert Greenvale smiled his pleasure. "I shall inform my aunt, ma'am. She will be delighted." He stood up to leave. "I look forward to seeing you this evening. Ladies, your servant. Coming, Sommerton . . . ?"

The two gentlemen went out together and Mrs Pollard turned to Arabella. "You have made a conquest, my dear. I have never seen Robert so taken with a pretty face!"

Arabella flushed. "I'm sure he was just being kind."

Catherine's eyes twinkled. "You need not pretend with me, my dear. I know your situation and I think you've made a wise choice. I happen to know Robert has decided to marry at last — he wants an heir before it's too late."

Arabella laughed. "So you think I

stand a chance of becoming Lady Greenvale?"

"If you carry on the way you've begun I should think you will be married as soon as you put off your blacks — a spring wedding would do nicely I should think."

Arabella smiled wickedly. "I was thinking the same . . . "

She suddenly remembered her last meeting with Seth. "Wait for me," he'd said and she had promised she would. She shut the memory out of her mind. He had lied to her: he was the father of Rose's child.

Because of her love for him she had given in to Christopher's blackmail. What a fool she had been! But now she knew men for what they were. A man wanted only one thing from a woman and from now on she would make them pay for their pleasure! She would take Lord Greenvale if he offered for her. And once she was his wife she would do exactly as she pleased!

Just as her father had once prophesied, Arabella rapidly became the latest rage. Wherever she went the gentlemen seemed to gravitate to her side. The lovely girl in the black gown drew all eyes, and her pale, sweet face was spoken of in reverent tones.

Inwardly she was amused by their eagerness to please her. What liars they were! Did they think she believed their flattery! Outwardly, she maintained a gentle dignity, graciously dispensing her favours to the young men who flocked around her: but she saved her smiles for Lord Greenvale.

Only Robert was permitted to take her driving in his carriage. It was he who read to her for hours, or watched while she sketched in Catherine's gardens during the mild autumn afternoons. And it was he who finally asked her to marry him two days before she returned home.

Arabella kept her eyes downcast so

that he should not see the sudden gleam of excitement in them. She twisted the pearl bracelet on her arm nervously, making him wait before she replied:

"You do me great honour, sir," she said at last. "You know I am still in mourning for my father — but if you were to speak to Philip at Christmas I am sure he would consent to an engagement."

Robert's face lit up. He took her hand and kissed it reverently. "You have made me the happiest of men, Arabella."

"My father always held a party at Christmastide," she said, allowing him to hold her hand for a moment. "Philip intends to continue the custom. I will ask him to invite you to stay; we could announce our betrothal at the party."

"Six weeks is a long time, Arabella. May I not come sooner?"

"I must have time to prepare my brother; he may be surprised I am thinking of marriage so soon after . . . "

"Forgive me, my dear. My love for you makes me forget your sad loss. I will wait until Christmas."

Arabella smiled at him. "You cannot be more impatient than I, Robert. You may kiss me if you wish."

"My dearest girl." He took her in his arms, kissing her very gently.

Arabella stood unmoving. She felt nothing; but she had not expected to. She was marrying him for his wealth not for love. For a moment she wondered if she could go through with it, but squashed her doubts. She had nothing to lose.

★ ★ ★

Philip whistled as Arabella told him he could expect to announce her engagement at Christmas. "How did you manage it, Bella? He must be the catch of the season!"

Arabella shrugged. "He was certainly the richest of my suitors."

Philip was disturbed by the hard note

in her voice. "I'm sorry it had to be this way, Bella."

Arabella laughed, her eyes brilliant. "Don't worry, Philip. I'm not doing it just for the estate."

"Are you in love with him?" Philip sounded hopeful.

"What has love to do with it? I shall have three houses, carriages, jewels: who needs love?"

Philip winced. Something had happened to Arabella. He did not understand it, and he did not much like the cold, sophisticated woman she had become.

Arabella smiled and for a moment he saw the mischievous child he had always loved. "Everything will be fine. I promise."

"If you say so, Bella."

"I do. Now I'm going riding."

"Shall I come?"

Arabella shook her head. "I want to be alone. We'll go out together another day."

"All right."

Philip watched her go. Something

was wrong. She had not been the same since their father died. Perhaps she was still grieving. He sighed. Whatever it was he couldn't reach her.

★ ★ ★

Arabella rode through the park. The sun was warm on her face, the weather so mild that it almost seemed summer had returned for a brief spell. It was good to be home again . . .

Arabella reined in suddenly as she saw the man coming through the trees, her heart leaping. In that moment she knew her love for Seth had not died, and she was furious at her own weakness. She should hate him: but she didn't. She slid from the saddle as he held his arms out to her.

"I hoped you would ride today. I came as soon as I heard you were home . . . " He looked at her face, realising she was angry. "What is wrong?"

Arabella felt the anger flare inside

her. She was torn between raking his face with her nails and throwing herself in his arms.

"How is Rose?" she asked coldly. "When are you to be married?"

He looked bewildered. "Why should I marry Rose?"

"Because you are the father of her child; she told me herself!"

Seth laughed. "Surely you didn't believe her!" His smile faded. "Damn it, Bella, Rose wouldn't know who the father was; there was scarcely a man in the village who wasn't eligible, except me. You're the only woman I want." His voice carried the ring of truth.

"Oh, Seth . . . " Arabella caught her breath. "Forgive me . . . "

"If Rose lied to you it was because she knew I loved you." He frowned. "Do you think I'd risk my neck for a woman I didn't love? If things go well for us I'll have the money tomorrow night. I've invested everything I've managed to beg, steal or smuggle into a cargo of my own."

Arabella stared at him. How on earth had he managed to get so much money so quickly? He must have taken untold risks. She was suddenly afraid for him, afraid of the dangers involved in landing a big cargo.

"Oh, Seth, what have I done to you?"

Seth drew her into his arms. "Don't cry, my darling. Nothing will happen to me: I bear a charmed life."

Arabella shook her head. What had she done? How could she hope to explain about Christopher Allingham? Seth would never forgive her . . .

She realised he was watching her, a puzzled look in his eyes. She couldn't tell him! He would feel betrayed as she had when she believed him the father of Rose's child. He might stop loving her: she couldn't bear that.

"I've missed you so much, Seth."

"My lovely Bella." His voice was suddenly hoarse with desire. "I want you so much . . . "

It was impossible to speak. Arabella

simply lifted her face to his, offering her lips. She felt him shudder as his arms went round her, and she clung to him.

Seth's big hands were incredibly gentle as he undressed her. He found the buttons of her bodice too tiny for his fingers, fumbling with them clumsily as the storm of emotion shook him.

"Damn it, Bella, I shall die of frustration!"

Arabella laughed huskily. "Let me, Seth, you're too impatient."

He laughed, releasing her while she took off her gown; but when she would have stepped out of her petticoats, he shook his head. She stood still as he removed the last pieces of her clothing, his eyes feasting hungrily on the creamy smoothness of her skin.

"Bella . . . " he whispered. "You're so lovely . . . so lovely . . . "

Seth was so gentle. She had never dreamed a big man could be this gentle. His hands were almost reverent as they touched her, as if he feared she would break. She pressed closer to him, feeling the burn of his strong thighs against hers, wanting him to possess her utterly.

She spread her legs wide for him, feeling him rocking against her as he tried to leash the fierce desire burning inside him. She pressed her lips to his throat, licking the salt sweat with the tip of her tongue.

"Love me, Seth," she whispered. "Love me now."

He moaned hoarsely, easing himself into her as if he feared to cause her pain. She stiffened with surprise as he entered her, feeling as much pain as the first time. She gasped and he held back as if he would leave her, but she held him against her tightly, arching her body to meet him.

It had never been like this with Christopher. Arabella was on fire with sensation, her whole body aflame with a searing white heat. Seth filled her completely. She could feel herself stretched taut around him. He was hurting her but it was a sweet, savage hurt. She wanted it to go on for ever!

The pleasure was so intense that she cried out, writhing wildly beneath him. Then she was shaken by a spasm of sheer ecstasy, as though something deep inside her had reached out to draw him even deeper into her.

She lay with her eyes closed, utterly satiated as he drew away from her, conscious only of her own happiness and the wonderful thing which had just happened to her. Exhausted, Arabella did not at first notice that something was wrong with Seth. It was only when she turned to him that she saw he was lying with his head buried in his arms, his whole body rigid with tension.

"What's wrong?" she asked, touching his shoulder.

He jerked away as though he'd been stung. She gazed into the black hell of his eyes and shivered.

"You know . . . "

"Who was it?"

"Does it matter?"

"I want to know!" Seth caught her wrist.

"Christopher Allingham."

His face worked with agony. "Were you in love with him?"

"No." Arabella stared at him miserably, knowing she could never explain. He would not believe her.

"Was it because of Rose?"

Arabella seized the excuse he offered. She nodded once, not looking at him.

He stood up and pulled on his breeches, his back turned to her. Arabella thought he meant to leave her. She threw herself at him, pressing her face against his thighs.

"Forgive me, Seth," she begged. "I love you . . . "

He looked down at her tear-stained face. "What choice have I? You're in my blood for good or evil but if you ever let another man touch you, God help me, I'll kill you!"

"I won't. I swear I won't!"

"Get up, Bella. You'd better get dressed."

Arabella dressed in silence, wishing he would say something — anything. "When shall I see you?"

"I'll meet you here on Sunday. Come on foot and bring nothing of value with you."

Arabella nodded. "Don't go like this, Seth. I'm sorry. So very sorry . . . "

The black eyes were full of an aching sadness which hurt her more than if he'd struck her. "I'll get over it but it may take a while."

Arabella turned her head away. "I must go," she said, her face pale. "Will you help me?"

"Of course."

Seth gave her his hand, tossing her up into the saddle with a careless ease. Arabella looked down at him. "Sunday," she said, then flicked the reins and turned her horse towards home.

She was completely unaware that Richard was watching her from the thicket — and that he had witnessed the whole of her meeting with Seth . . .

★ ★ ★

Arabella went quickly up to her room, not wanting anyone to see her before she changed her gown. There were damp stains on the skirt and her hair was tangled. Besides, she wanted to be alone so that she could think.

Everything had changed when Seth made love to her; all the bitterness of the past months had drained out of her and she knew she would always love him. Closing her eyes, she saw again the pain in his face as he learned the truth of her betrayal. Would he ever forgive her?

"Oh, Seth, my love, forgive me . . . " she whispered, tears choking her. "I did not want to go to him . . . I did not want to betray you . . . "

She began to strip off her clothes, padding across to the washstand to pour cool water into a basin. As she washed her body all over in the refreshing water, her thoughts returned to Seth. Somehow she had to win back

111

his trust and love. She meant to keep her promise to him. She would be a good wife to him . . .

Arabella turned in surprise as the door of her room opened, catching up her shift against her naked body as Richard came in. She gasped as she saw him lock the door and put the key in his waistcoat pocket.

"Richard — what are you doing? Get out of here!"

Richard ignored her demand. He walked purposefully towards her, his eyes blazing with anger as he reached out and snatched the shift away.

"Why so modest, Bella?" he snarled. "You were eager enough to strip yourself for Seth Blackthorn!"

Arabella drew a sharp breath, the colour draining from her face as she saw the insane glitter in his eyes. She felt a thrill of fear shoot through her. This man was a stranger, someone she had never seen before.

"Well?" he asked. "Have you nothing to say?"

Arabella lifted her head proudly. "What should I say, Richard? I'm going to marry Seth, and nothing you can do or say will stop me."

"No?"

Anger blazed out of Richard suddenly. The fury of the blow which sent her staggering against the bedpost surprised Arabella, but she raised her head defiantly, shaking her mane of pale gold hair away from her face, her eyes proud. She refused to let him see her pain. Then her defiance turned to shock and incredulity as she saw him fumbling with his breeches and a terrible suspicion dawned in her mind.

"What are you doing?" she whispered. "Richard you can't! You're my brother . . ."

For answer he hit her again. She began to scream, struggling wildly as he forced her backwards over the edge of the bed. He snatched up her shift, stuffing the fine material into her mouth to stifle her cries. One arm was thrust across her throat, pinioning her to the bed and effectively terminating her struggles. The constricting pressure of his forearm made it difficult to breathe. She went limp beneath him.

"Lie still, you bitch," Richard snarled. "Or I'll hurt you even more."

Arabella had no choice but to obey, enduring the mental and physical agony of rape in a numbed silence. But through it all she was aware that Richard took a savage delight in abusing her body. At last he slumped against her with a grunt of animal satisfaction.

Arabella lay still, too shocked to move even when she felt him leave her. She closed her eyes, refusing to look at him, though she was sickeningly aware of him standing beside the bed.

"Look at me!"

Arabella moved her head negatively, too shamed to obey. She was jerked roughly to a sitting position, his fingers biting into her shoulders cruelly as he shook her.

"I said look at me!"

She opened her eyes dully.

"That's better. Listen to me, Bella. I'm going now, and I shall lock the door behind me. If anyone comes you're not well. Do you understand me? You want to be left alone."

"I understand." Arabella's voice was toneless.

"I haven't finished with you yet," Richard said as he released her. "That was just a taste of what you're going to get. If you act like a whore, you must expect to be treated like one."

As he reached the door, Richard suddenly paused and looked back at her, his face twisted in an ugly sneer. "In case you thought of escaping through the secret passage, I've secured it from the other side."

Arabella hardly heard his taunt. She slumped back on the pillows, closing her eyes. She lay there unmoving even after he went out of the room, locking the door behind him.

★ ★ ★

It was a perfect night for the 'Gentlemen'. Cold and crisp with a touch of frost, the skies were velvet dark and lit only by a sprinkling of stars. The absence of a moon would cover the furtive activities of the small boats as they rowed out to the French ship riding at anchor in the cove, returning loaded down with their precious cargoes of silks, laces, tobacco and brandy.

Most of the contraband had already been unloaded and was being strapped on the backs of the pack horses as Seth pulled towards the shore with the last boatload. The steady plop of the oars and the gentle swish of the water against the sides of the boat were the only sounds to be heard as the French ship began to weigh anchor.

It had been doubly dangerous to bring the Frenchie in so close to shore, increasing the risk of discovery. It was easier to trade with the men of the Scilly Isles who took their long boats to the French coast and brought back small cargoes to sell. But Seth was in a hurry: he wanted a full cargo bought and paid for with his own money.

Arrangements had already been made for the disposal of the goods. They had only to lead the horses through the narrow lanes of Sussex to a certain flint-walled barn some ten miles inland. When the barrels were stowed their part of the dangerous transaction was over. The barn belonged to a man of impeccable character. It was he who would sell the goods. He would pay the agreed sum in gold when the contraband was delivered. They had worked together before to everyone's satisfaction.

The French ship was already putting out to sea when Seth's boat beached. He jumped over the side, wading into the shallows as two of the others came to help him drag the boat clear of the water. They were unloading the last of the barrels when the shout went up.

One of the smugglers was pointing out towards the bay. Seth swore violently as he saw the white sails of the

Revenue cutter and heard the warning shot she put across the Frenchman's bows. Then another ship sailed into view from the opposite direction. They were trying to bottle the French ship up, preventing her from reaching the open sea.

But the French captain was an experienced seaman. He brought his ship round on a new tack setting it straight at the Revenue cutter. It looked as if the two ships were on a collision course; but at the last moment the Frenchman tacked again zigzagging past the rocks which stretched out in spears from the cliffs.

The captain of the Revenue cutter had brought his vessel round sharply to avoid the collision, believing the Frenchman would not dare to go in too close to the rocks. He had left a narrow channel, and though the English guns belched flame and smoke, the French ship did not falter. She sailed cheekily past the astounded Revenue cutter heading for deep water, and soon began to draw away from her persuers.

The ragged cheer from the men on shore died as soldiers suddenly poured onto the pebbled beach. The smugglers fled in panic, leaving the contraband scattered on the sand.

Seth stood his ground as the scarlet-coated dragoon charged straight at him. Then, as the soldier raised his sword to strike, he bent and scooped up a stone from the beach, hurling it with all his strength. It struck the soldier in the middle of his forehead, splitting his flesh wide open. His sword dropped to the ground as he slumped forward over his horses' neck.

Seth picked up the sword as two more dragoons bore down on him. He side-stepped the first charge, slashing at the man's legs as he swept past, then turned to meet a fresh attack. But even as he did so a shot rang out. The ball creased his temple; everything went black and he pitched forward into the sand.

★ ★ ★

Arabella opened her eyes as she heard the scrape of a key turning. She stiffened as Richard came in carrying a lighted candle and a tray of food.

She sat up warily, holding the covers against her as she watched him lock the door behind him.

Richard stood looking down at her, his eyes glittering. "I've brought you some food: we don't want you to starve. Philip tells me you're going to restore the family fortunes by marrying Lord Greenvale: what a clever girl you are!"

Arabella hugged her knees, trying to control her trembling limbs. Richard was mad: he had to be! She remembered the mystery surrounding his mother's death, recalling scraps of gossip she'd dismissed as servant's tales: now they began to make sense.

"Leave me alone, Richard," she pleaded. "I won't tell Philip if you let me go now."

Richard smiled, his nostrils flaring. "But I haven't finished with you yet, my lovely sister."

He reached out and yanked the bedcovers from her. She shrank away from him, her eyes dark with horror. "No — not again. Please, Richard, not again!"

His fingers tore at the silk of her nightgown, ripping it. He began to caress her breasts, pinching the nipples as she tried to push his hands away. She cried out in pain and he slapped her face. Then he caught her wrists above her head, pinioning her to the bed.

"Lie still unless you want me to hurt you," he warned, bending his head to kiss her.

Arabella tried to twist away, but he held her fast. His feverish lips moved lingeringly down her throat, burning her. She stiffened as he began to kiss her breasts. This was even worse than the brutal rape of last night: he was behaving like a lover.

She looked up into his face, seeing the blind passion there. "Richard . . ." she whispered. "Don't do this to me — please."

"Smile at me, Bella," he said hoarsely. "Come to me of your own free will — let me have you the way you were with him."

Arabella felt the vomit rise in her throat. She twisted sideways, retching and spewing up the bitter bile. The acrid stench of her vomit caused Richard to release her. He stood watching for a moment, then walked to the washstand and poured some water into a basin. He soaked a cloth in it and gave it to her.

Arabella took it from him, wiping her mouth and suddenly realising she was no longer afraid of him. "How long have you felt like this?" she asked. "It wasn't just to punish me last night, was it?"

Richard shook his head. "I tried not to think about it," he said slowly. "For years I thought it was just the natural love of a brother for his sister, but then — then I began to dream of holding you in my arms and making love to you. I knew it was wrong. I hated myself for even thinking of such a thing — but when I discovered you had given yourself to Allingham the dreams became more vivid: they haunted me. I couldn't help myself, Bella — I love you . . . "

Arabella made a sound of disbelief. "Is that why you raped me?"

Richard's face was grey. All the aggression seemed to have drained out of him and he sagged against the bedpost. "I must have been out of my mind. I didn't mean it to happen."

"Don't lie, Richard. You knew just what you were doing; you intended it to happen again tonight."

"You hate me, don't you?"

"Yes."

For a moment Richard's eyes reflected his despair then they flickered with anger. "You might as well have something more to hate me for . . . "

His face hardened. "Seth Blackthorn was killed tonight. He murdered a Revenue officer and they shot him. I was listening when he told you about the drop. I knew the cove was used for smuggling — I told the Revenue men where they could find him . . . "

Arabella blanched. "No," she whispered. Then, her voice rising to a scream: "You're lying! You think you can keep me from him. But I will go to him — I will!"

Richard unlocked the door, then he turned back to her with a strange, tortured look in his eyes. "You are free to go where you please — I hope you rot in Hell, you little slut!"

He went out, leaving the door open. Arabella flew to it, slamming it shut and locking it. His words had shocked her out of her apathy. He was lying when he said Seth was dead. Dear Heaven, he had to be. He had to be!

She leaned against the door, shaking all over as she tried to think what to do now. Somehow she must learn the truth of tonight's happenings, because she could not, would not, believe Richard.

Seth could not be dead. Oh, please let Richard be lying. She could not bear it if Seth was dead.

★ ★ ★

Molly was sitting in her chair by the fire when Arabella burst in. She was pale and drawn, her eyes ringed with red. She looked at Arabella without surprise.

"So you've heard then."

Arabella stared, shaking her head as the fear swept through her. "Tell me he isn't dead!"

Molly saw her distress and some of the hostility went out of her. "We don't know for sure. They took his body with them, but we don't know where. His father has gone to the village to find out what he can."

"May I wait until he returns? Please let me stay, Molly. I have to know."

"Aye, I suppose you do." She studied

Arabella's face. "I knew he was going out with the gentlemen. I begged him to stop before it was too late. We've a good life here — we didn't need more than we have. But it was for you he wanted the money. He told me he was going away with you. I didn't really believe it until now . . . "

Arabella shivered. "Don't look at me that way, Molly. You can't hate me more than I hate myself." She broke off on a sob. "Oh, Molly, I love him. What shall I do if . . . ?"

"You'll bear it, lass, same as we all will. Still, there's no sense in fretting afore we know for sure." She stood up. "We'll have some tea: one of Seth's presents to me since he started running with the gentlemen. He was always a good boy . . . "

Motioning Arabella to a chair, she began to move about the kitchen, setting the big iron kettle over the fire and taking out the delicate cups and saucers which had been Lady Pennington's wedding gift to her.

Arabella had a wild desire to laugh, cry or scream; but she couldn't decide which. How could she sit drinking tea when Seth was missing? She couldn't bear the waiting. But even as she jumped to her feet in an agony of suspense, the door opened and Seth's father came in.

"There's no news . . . " he began, breaking off with a growl of anger as he saw Arabella. "What's she doing here?"

"She came to ask about Seth."

"I want her out of my house!"

He moved threateningly towards Arabella, but Molly caught his arm. "You've no call to take against the lass, Tom, she loves him."

He snorted his disgust. "Her kind wouldn't know how!"

Arabella looked at him, her face white. "I know you hate me, and I'll go as soon as you've told me what has happened to Seth."

He scowled at her, then shook his head wearily. "No one knows. Several men saw him fall but dare not go back to investigate. They think he may be alive, otherwise the body would probably have been left on the beach as a warning."

Arabella's eyes lit up. "Then he must be alive. Oh, thank God!"

"What good will it do him if he is? He'll hang for killing a Revenue officer — that's why they took him."

"We'll find a way." Arabella looked at him eagerly. "A lawyer . . . "

Tom growled low in his throat. "You don't know what you're saying. 'Tis not just the smuggling: he's a murderer! Even if we had the money it would be useless."

Arabella saw the scorn in his eyes. She lifted her head proudly. "If you can discover where he's been taken I will do the rest."

"What can you do? Your estate is mortgaged to the hilt; you'll be lucky to have a roof over your heads by next summer."

"Tom!" Molly looked shocked.

"There are ways," Arabella said,

deliberately echoing Seth's own words. "There are ways of finding the money, even for someone like me."

Tom glared at her. "I'll not ask for your help."

Arabella walked to the door, glancing back at Molly. "I shall not come again," she said quietly.

"Miss Arabella!" Molly cried in protest.

"Let her go, woman: we don't want her kind."

Arabella smiled at Molly. Her mind was clear as she went out into the crisp air. She would write to Lord Greenvale begging him to come as soon as he could. Once she was Lady Greenvale she would pay someone to help her discover Seth's whereabouts. Nothing mattered to her now except finding him.

* * *

It was light when Seth came to himself. He was lying on something hard, his

129

head was throbbing and his tongue was so dry that it stuck to the roof of his mouth.

"Water," he croaked. "Water . . . "

"Woke up 'ave you, mate?" a cheerful voice asked and a face swam mistly before Seth's eyes.

An arm was slipped beneath his shoulders and he was lifted sufficiently to gulp a mouthful of the tepid water. He swallowed greedily but the cup was withdrawn.

"Not too much at a time, matey. You've bin out for a couple of days: best to take it steady for a while I reckon."

"Thank you."

Seth lay back with a sigh. Running his fingers up to the ache in his temple he discovered a crude bandage. He tried to remember what had happened, groaning as the pieces clicked into place. He sat up, his head spinning.

"Steady on, mate! You ain't up to it yet."

Seth blinked. The mist was clearing

now; he could see the face of his companion. It was the weatherbeaten face of a sailor. The man grinned, revealing a row of rotten teeth as Seth climbed unsteadily to his feet, towering above him. "Cor, you're a big'un, ain't you? No wonder it took three of 'em to carry you in!"

Seth made a grimace that might have been a smile. "Where are we? And who are you?"

"Somewhere near Rye I reckon." The little man laughed. "Me name's Rotten Willie; and don't let them choppers fool you. I was born bad so me ma said. Theivin', smuggling, slave running, all the same to me. This time I went too far, killed a man over a wench." He drew his finger across his throat. "I reckon it's curtains for me."

"Then we're in the same boat, Willie. I killed a Revenue man." He held out his hand. "I'm Seth Blackthorn."

Rotten Willie wiped his hands on his stained breeches. His palms were clammy with sweat, and Seth realised he was actually shaking with fear. He wasn't in that state himself as yet, but hanging was not a pleasant thought. He began to take stock of his surroundings, noting the high windows and the thick door.

He looked at Willie. "If you stood on my shoulders you could see what it's like outside."

"Mebbe — what's the point?"

Seth grinned. "The point is, my friend, that if we're where I think we might be, this place is part of an old abbey. They used it to put Frenchies in during the last war — one of them told me about it."

Willie stared. "If you're thinking what I think you're thinking . . . "

"I am." Seth's mouth hardened. "I don't intend to wait here until they decide to hang me. You can come or stay as you please."

The little man hawked and spat on the ground. "I'm your man, Captain, just show me the way."

Seth laughed. "You can start by

looking out of the window."

He knelt down and Willie hopped on his shoulders with the agility of a man used to climbing a ship's rigging. Seth stood up and walked to the window, his strong hands gripping the little man's calves.

"What am I supposed to see?"

"Just some ruined walls — oh, and a tree. There should be an oak tree."

"Ain't no tree, nothin' except a pile of old stones."

"Right, that's exactly right," Seth said excitedly. "You can come down now." He bent and Willie slid to the ground.

"Weren't no tree," he said. "How can you be sure it's the same place?"

"It has to be," Seth's voice was grim. "It doesn't matter about the tree, maybe you can't see it from this part of the building. Besides, look at the writing on the wall, that's French."

"Here — you feelin' all right?" Willie asked as Seth's face went grey.

"My head hurts. I've got to lie down

for a while." He grinned as he saw Willie's look. "Don't worry, I'm not dying. I need to think and I'll do it better lying down — but I could do with some more of that water."

Willie looked relieved. "Sure thing, Captain, anything you say goes with me . . . "

4

AS Arabella entered the drawing room, Lord Greenvale left Philip standing by the fireplace and came to greet her, hands outstretched.

"How happy I was to receive your letter, my dear. I came at once."

Arabella lifted her cheek for him to kiss. "I found it impossible to wait, Robert."

She flushed as she saw the look of adoration he gave her, feeling guilty. He was a decent man and what she was doing was unfair to him, but nothing mattered to her now except Seth.

Arabella glanced at Philip, who responded with a smile. "Everything is arranged. We are agreed on a Christmas wedding — if you feel you can be ready by then, Bella?"

"Oh yes. I shan't bother with a

trousseau. I can buy new gowns in Town later."

"You shall have all the gowns you desire, and you can choose them in Paris if you wish." Lord Greenvale looked at her fondly. "You have only to ask for what you desire."

Arabella lowered her long lashes. She longed to demand his instant assistance in discovering Seth's whereabouts, but knew she dare not do so yet. It must be a casual request, made on behalf of Seth's mother.

No one must guess how much it meant to her personally.

Richard knew the truth and she was terrified he would try to stop her if he knew what she intended. He had been avoiding her since that night, and she knew he was drinking heavily, returning in the early hours after spending the night with some of his wilder friends. She was glad he seemed to avoid her: she could scarcely bear to look at him these days.

Richard may have been ashamed

of what he'd done, Arabella had no way of knowing, nor even if he was aware of the enormity of his crime. Sometimes she believed the balance of his mind was disturbed, and then she dismissed the idea. Richard was not mad: he'd known just what he was doing! For herself she had buried the pain and horror of that night in some far corner of her mind where it could not touch her.

She knew now that Richard's mother had taken her own life after having been depressed for some time: Aunt Augusta had reluctantly told her the truth. So there was an inherited weakness in Richard, though Philip seemed to have been spared it. And yet Arabella could not accept that Richard's action had been that of a madman. She might have found it easier to understand if he were really ill.

Sometimes she thought that his cruelty would prevent her finding natural joy in the arms of a man again; then the longing for Seth would start up inside her once more and she felt it would be all right if she could be with him. Of the price she must first pay to obtain his freedom she refused to think at all.

She had no choice but to go through with the marriage. Tom had said there was nothing to be done, but Arabella was sure there must be some way of helping Seth. Turnkeys and even judges could be bribed if the sum was large enough — and with Lord Greenvale's fortune at her command she could pay their price.

She smiled at Robert, feeling a stab of guilt as he slipped a large sapphire and diamond ring on her finger, promising herself she would return it when she went away with Seth. She wanted nothing for herself, only as much as it took to buy Seth's freedom.

"It's beautiful; thank you," she said. "It's kind of you to offer to take me to Paris but I should prefer to stay in England for a while."

He kissed her hand. "We will do

whatever pleases you, my dear."

"Then we shall stay in England. Would you care for a walk around the gardens before dinner?" She withdrew her hand from his. "Wait one moment while I send for my cloak . . . "

★ ★ ★

Seth lay with his eyes closed, listening to the steady tread of the turnkey's feet. Any moment now he would pause outside their cell and push the meagre rations of food and water through a small opening at the bottom of the door. Somehow he had to be persuaded to come inside!

Suddenly Rotten Willie started hammering on the door, his eyes rolling from side to side and yelling at the top of his voice. "Let me out! I ain't gonna stop in 'ere all night with a stiff. For Christsake, let me out!"

The turnkey stopped, peering suspiciously through the bars. "Are you sure he's dead?"

"For gawd's sake get him outta 'ere afore I go barmy."

"Can't shift him on me own," grumbled the turnkey. "I'll fetch Alf. Calm down, man, he can't hurt you." He shot Willie a look of dislike as the little man began to yell again. It was bad enough having a corpse to deal with let alone a raving lunatic.

He went off at a run to fetch his comrade. Willie winked at Seth, stuffing a lump of bread inside his shirt. Food wasn't easy to come by on the run. Seth held out his hand for the cup of water, but Willie motioned him to lie still.

"They're comin' back," he hissed, beginning to hammer on the door again.

The gaoler slid a key into the lock, warning Willie to move out of the way. "And no tricks from you," he growled. "Alf here's got a mean way with him."

"I ain't no troublemaker," Willie was almost weeping now. "Just get that stiff outta 'ere, will you!"

Alf walked over to where Seth was lying, peering at his face. "Don't look dead to me," he began as Seth's hand snaked out and gripped his ankle. "Hey!"

The next moment his legs were jerked from under him and he crashed to the floor. In an instant Seth had straddled him, hitting him just once on the jaw. He grunted and went limp.

Almost at the same moment Willie plunged a jagged shaft of metal into the turnkey's back. Seth whirled round as he heard the man's scream.

"There was no need to kill him. I would have dealt with him soon enough."

"Not before he raised the alarm. Anyway, what's it matter?" Willie spat on the dead man's body. "Let's get outta 'ere afore any more of 'em come."

"Take his keys; they'll open the outer doors for us." Seth bent over Alf's unconscious body, slipping the pistol from his belt. "We may need this if they heard that scream."

Willie tore the keys from the dead man's hand, swearing as even in death he seemed reluctant to part with them. He followed Seth out of the cell and along the flint-walled passage. The sound of laughter reached them; and at a sign from Seth, Willie dropped to his knees. They crawled past the guardroom, hearing the rough voices of the men inside. They had reached the outer door when the shouting began.

"Oh, gawd, one of 'em must have found 'im," Willie said, his skin turning grey. "For Christsakes get that door open, Captain!"

Seth had been unhurriedly trying the keys one by one. He grinned as the door swung open. "Come on then — what are you waiting for? Make for the wall; I'll help you over it."

Willie threw him a scared glance and ran. He scrabbled for footholds in the rough stone wall, then found himself lifted high enough so that he could grab the edge and hang on. He pulled himself on to it, half-lying on the sharp flints on top, watching as Seth confidently began the climb. Then he yelled, "They're coming!"

Seth glanced over his shoulder. He heaved himself up and straddled the wall before dropping to the other side. Willie hesitated, then came slithering down to join him.

"Follow me and keep close," Seth commanded, and Willie obeyed with a blind faith born of his terror. The Captain knew where he was going; at least Willie prayed he did!

They were running through what was almost a wasteland of rough grass and furze bushes, nothing higher than waistlevel and no sign of any shelter. They could hear shouting behind them and two shots rang out. Neither found their mark, and the fugitives kept on running.

Now Willie could smell the unmistakable tang of the sea, and he saw they were actually on top of what seemed to be a plateau jutting out into nothing but sky, and a long drop to the rocks below. He glanced over his shoulder and yelled as he saw two horsemen in pursuit.

Seth stopped running for a moment, recovering his breath and getting his bearings. Then he started to run again.

Willie followed closely. "Where we goin', Captain?"

" Over the edge of course."

Willie stopped abruptly. "I reckon I'd sooner take my chance back there."

"Trust me."

The horsemen were catching up with them. A shot passed perilously close to Willie's head. He gave a squawk of terror and set out after Seth again in a hurry.

Seth had halted by a large flat stone. He appeared to be pacing out the distance from it to the edge of the cliff. Then, before Willie's disbelieving eyes, he suddenly disappeared over the side.

Willie yelled, running to the spot he'd last seen Seth. There was nothing in front of him but the sky and a sheer fall of cliff to the foaming water below.

"Where are you, Captain?" he quavered. "Don't leave me."

"Come on, Willie."

Seth's head appeared out of the side of the rock a few feet below the edge. Willie saw there was a deep crack running through the face of the cliff wide enough for a man to enter. Jutting out from the sheer face was a spur of rock just large enough for a foothold, clearly the only way in.

"I can't, Captain. I can't do it."

"Lie down flat and wriggle over the edge backwards. When you feel my hands on your legs just let yourself go."

Willie still hesitated, looking down at the grey water swirling below. Then another shot passed over his head and he threw himself on the ground. The sweat was pouring from his forehead as he inched himself backwards, scrabbling for a foothold; then he felt a firm hand grip his shin. He let go, slithering down into the gulley like a little lizard. He was hauled bodily into the cave and set on his feet.

"Thanks, Captain," he muttered.

"We're not out of trouble yet." Seth frowned. "If we can do it so can they — and I've no way of knowing how far these passages wind on for."

Willie looked fearfully into the dark interior of the cave. "We ain't goin' in there, are we?"

"Cheer up, Willie. Remember I told you about those French prisoners of war I met up with? Well, we had some time to kill while we were waiting for the tide to change and one of them described how he'd escaped from this place. He made it, why shouldn't we?"

Willie gulped. "Lead on then, Captain. Where are we headin' when we get out of here?"

"Once we are at the other end we'll both go our own ways."

"I'm for a ship myself. England won't be safe for a while. Why don't you come with me?"

Seth's face was grim. "There's something I must do first."

"If you change your mind you'll find me at the Fishy Tale in Portsmouth — until I get a ship."

"I'll remember," Seth said. "Watch your step, the floor of the cave falls away sharply here . . . "

★ ★ ★

Arabella was sitting at her desk in the library when Charis came in. She signed her letter with a flourish, sanded it and folded it neatly, adding it to the pile in front of her. Then she turned to Charis with a sigh of relief.

"I think that's the last of the invitations. I never realised getting married was such hard work."

Charis looked concerned. "You look tired, have you not been sleeping well?"

"Perhaps not."

Arabella sighed and stood up. She knew it was not tiredness which ailed her but her growing anxiety. Why had no one heard anything of Seth? Desperation had driven her into making inquiries in the village herself. She realised that she was laying herself open to gossip, but she no longer cared what people thought of her. It was more than ten days now since Seth was shot, where was he? Oh, God, where was he?

She tried to smile at Charis. "I'm bored with being indoors — shall we go for a walk?"

Charis laughed. "That's why I came to find you. Philip has taken Lord Greenvale on a tour of the estate. I thought we might walk to meet them."

Charis was looking a little conscious. Arabella stared at her, sensing her excitement. "Why, Charis, I do believe Philip has proposed at last!"

Charis smiled shyly. "Yes — but only after I practically proposed to him. He thought I was in love with Richard!"

"I'm glad you're not." Arabella shuddered.

"I thought you might be cross with me because I chose Philip and not Richard. Did you know Richard asked me to marry him?"

"No. I thought he might, but I was sure you would refuse. You're much better off with Philip."

Charis looked awkward. "Have you quarrelled with Richard, Bella?"

Arabella turned her face aside. "Yes — but I would rather not talk about it if you don't mind."

"Of course not. Shall we go for our walk now?"

Arabella nodded, smiling a little too brightly. "Yes, I'll just fetch my cloak."

★ ★ ★

Seth flattened himself against the wall of the barn as the huge door swung back, preparing to attack. Then he drew a sigh of relief: it was only his father. He stepped forward, letting the light from Tom's lantern fall across his face.

Tom stared at his son. "Aye, I thought it might be you. How long have you been here?"

"Since early this morning."

"Why didn't you come to the house?"

"I'm a wanted man. I'll not endanger you and Molly. I only came to get something I left here. I'll be gone before morning."

"Without seeing your mother?"

"I'll send word when I can." Seth sighed as he saw his father's frown. "Why upset her for nothing? You know I can't stay here now."

"Mebbe you're right." Tom looked at the livid scar on Seth's forehead. "Seems you were lucky this time. What will you do now?"

"I'm not sure — I might go to France . . . " Seth held out his hand tentively. "I've let you down, haven't I?"

Tom ignored his hand. "Nay, I'll not

forgive you for breaking Molly's heart and shaming me. You were a fool, Seth. You had a good life and you threw it away for a little whore who was laughing at you all the time."

"What do you mean?" Seth snarled, his fists clenching.

"She's getting married, to some lord or other. She couldn't even wait to find out if you were still alive, that's how much she cared about you!"

"Damn you for that!"

Seth hit out wildly in his pain, felling his father with a blow to the chin. The older man lay on the ground shaking his head, looking at him scornfully. Seth groaned as he realised what he'd done.

"I'm sorry. I shouldn't have done that."

"You had the right." Tom got to his feet. "You had to be told."

"Don't expect me to thank you."

"I won't." Tom reached inside his shirt and took out a small package. "I brought some food in case it was you.

151

I shan't expect to find you here in the morning."

Seth took the package. "I'll be gone before then. Tell Molly I love her."

Tom stared at him. "Mebbe. Mebbe I'll tell her you're dead." He opened the barn door and went out into the night without a backward glance.

Seth stared at the door, wanting to hurl something at it in his rage and frustration. Until this moment he'd been nursing the faint hope that Bella might be willing to come with him. He'd hidden some money in the barn in case the landing went wrong: as it had. He was sure someone had betrayed him to the Revenue, but who? Only one man had known the precise time and location of the drop besides those on the beach. But he would surely have waited until the goods were safely stowed in his own barns if he'd wanted to double-cross Seth. No, there was no reason why he should have done it. He'd lost the vast profit he stood to make from the deal.

Only one other person knew of his plans: Arabella. Seth could hardly believe she was capable of such treachery, but his father had supplied the answer. The money he'd promised her had not been enough. She wanted something he could never give her. She wanted wealth and position: marriage to a man of her own class.

If it was true then she was a cold-hearted bitch and he was well rid of her. And yet the longing to hold her in his arms still burned in his guts, tearing at him. He had to see her again if only to tell her how much he despised her.

He stuffed the pouch of gold into his shirt, opening the parcel of food his father had brought and ripping off a lump of bread with his teeth. He would eat first and then decide what to do.

★ ★ ★

The room was full of people. Aunt Augusta had arranged the dinner party to announce Charis's engagement. It was the type of party Arabella always found boring; the guests were stuffy, old-fashioned friends of her aunt, most of whom she cordially disliked.

Arabella watched the four players at the card table, shaking her head as Charis offered to give up her place. Nothing on this earth would induce her to sit down and play cards with Richard.

For some reason he'd decided to stay in this evening, and he'd gone out of his way to be pleasant to Lord Greenvale. Arabella was suspicious, fearing he was planning some mischief; but she could scarcely forbid her future husband to play cards with her own brother.

She stood up, restless and uneasy. "I have a headache," she announced. "I think I shall go to my room and lie down for a while."

Lord Greenvale laid down his cards. "Is there anything I can do for you, my dear?"

"No, thank you. Please go on with

your game. I shall come down later if I feel better."

"Sit down, Greenvale, you can't leave in the middle of a game." Richard sounded irritated. "Bella will be all right, won't you?"

"Yes," Arabella's voice was stifled. She had to get out of this room or she would go mad! "Goodnight, everyone."

Arabella left hastily. She needed to be alone, and the headache was only an excuse. At the foot of the stairs she hesitated, then ran quickly up to her room. Putting on her cloak, she went back down the stairs and out of the house.

Despite the late hour it was quite light, a pale moon turning the trees to silver against the cloudless sky. Arabella breathed deeply, inhaling the crisp air as she turned towards the park. The night held no terrors for her. She loved its solitude.

She walked slowly, deep in thought, letting the silence enfold her. So intense was her longing that when the tall figure moved from behind a tree to confront her she thought she was dreaming.

"Hello, Arabella."

"Seth . . . " She stared at him in stunned disbelief. "Is it really you? Seth . . . "

She flew at him, flinging her arms around him in a rush of incredulous joy. Laughing, she lifted her face for his kiss; then she saw the look in his eyes and her heart stood still.

"Why are you staring at me like that?"

He caught her left wrist, lifting her hand so that the magnificent ring on her finger flashed in the moonlight. "So it was true," he said bitterly. "I hoped he was wrong, but I should've known. You bitch! You cheating, little bitch!"

Arabella gasped. "No, Seth, no! You don't understand. It was for you. I needed to get money to help you . . . "

"I don't believe you," he grated. "And even if I did, do you think I'd want that? I'd rather hang. Is that all it means to you, Bella, will you sell yourself to any man willing to pay the price? Allingham, me — God knows how many more!"

"No, please don't, Seth," she whimpered, tears sliding down her cheeks. "I love you . . ."

"Love! You don't know the meaning of the word."

The bitterness and scorn in Seth's voice stung her like the lash of a whip. She recoiled from him, shaking her head. Then she suddenly turned and fled, leaving him staring after her.

"Bella . . ."

The pain in his guts was ripping him apart. Half of him wanted to run after her and beg her forgiveness. The other half held him chained to the ground, torn and bleeding deep inside himself.

* * *

Arabella was sobbing as she ran, filled with a wild despair that made her want to keep on running for ever. How could

Seth say such terrible things to her? Hadn't she paid over and over again for her mistake? How she had paid! Men were all the same: vile and cruel, arrogant and selfish! At this moment she hated them all. Most of all she hated Richard.

Richard had betrayed Seth to the Revenue. Now Seth hated her, blaming her for that betrayal, but she was innocent. And she loved him, she loved him. He was as cruel as all the others, but she couldn't stop wanting him. She loved him so much she couldn't bear to go on living with the knowledge of his hatred.

Arabella's crazed flight had carried her through the park to the formal flower gardens. Beyond the neat flower beds and the ionic temple the lake gleamed silver in the moonlight. She ran towards it, intent on ending her life. Then they would all be sorry. She would like to make them suffer, all those who had combined to cause her pain. But Richard wouldn't be sorry. Richard had raped her — her own brother! Richard had betrayed Seth. Richard was the one who should die . . .

Arabella suddenly stood still, uncaring of the biting wind pulling at her clothes and whipping her golden hair across her face. She shuddered, her chest heaving as the blind, hot panic which had set her running hardened into a cold knot in her stomach. Icy shivers ran up and down her spine as she realised what she must do. Richard should die. He deserved to die!

She turned and began to walk towards the house. She was no longer in a hurry, her mind was very clear. She knew exactly what she was going to do. She entered the front door, ignoring the startled look of a servant hovering in the hall, unaware of how strange she looked, her hair wild and wind-blown, her eyes staring fixedly.

She walked slowly up the stairs to her room. Pulling open the top drawer of her chest, she lifted the piles of silk scarves and gloves. It was still where she'd placed it, the walnut box containing the silver-handled pistol her father had given her on her sixteenth birthday. She'd called it a pretty toy, preferring to use Sir William's duelling pistols when they practised together.

"It's still a lethal weapon, Bella," her father had said. "So use it wisely."

Arabella opened the box, taking out the tiny pistol and loading it with practised ease. Then she turned and went back down the stairs, the pistol partially concealed in the folds of her gown. Her face was pale but she felt quite calm.

They had finished playing cards when she returned to the drawing room. Charis was presiding over the tea-tray with the vicar's wife beside her and Aunt Augusta on the settee. Colonel Braybrooke and Lord Greenvale were talking together while Philip was at a desk in the far corner of the room. Richard was standing by the fireplace staring moodily into the flames, his back turned to her.

"Oh good, you're feeling better, Bella."

Arabella gave no sign of having heard Charis speak. She was staring at Richard, unconscious of all eyes suddenly turned upon her. She called Richard's name. He turned to look at her and she saw he had a glass of blood red wine in his hand. The colour seemed to mist before her eyes, filling her vision. She raised her pistol, pointing it at a spot just above his heart.

Richard's face went grey, his eyes bulging. "Bella . . . Bella, no . . . "

Charis half-rose in her seat, her eyes wide with shock. "Bella — Richard . . . " she whispered, stunned. She screamed as Arabella fired.

The glass fell from Richard's hand, sending a deep, dark stain spreading through the carpet. He seemed startled, a look of surprise in his eyes. Momentarily he hung suspended in space, staring at her. Then his body crumpled and he

161

sank slowly to his knees. His eyes met hers briefly, then he pitched forward on to his face.

Arabella dropped the pistol on the floor. "I'm going to my room," she said. "I shall be there when I'm wanted."

★ ★ ★

Seth stood outside the inn, looking up at the sign swaying back and forth in the wind. It portrayed a beautiful mermaid, and underneath the legend: The Fishy Tale. He grimaced and went in.

Inside the inn was even more seedy than it appeared from outside. The stench of stale wine and sweat met his nostrils, making him pause. The room was full of rough-looking seamen and loud-voiced women. In one corner two harridans were screaming and fighting over a sailor who swayed drunkenly between them.

Seth's mouth curled with distaste and he turned to leave; he was in no mood for this. He'd made a mistake in coming here. He would find a decent place to stay overnight and in the morning he would take the first ship for France. He was about to leave when he heard a shout and Willie came pushing through the crowd towards him.

"By all that's wonderful — it's the Captain! Come on I'll buy you a drink."

Seth almost refused Willie's invitation, then shrugged his shoulders. He was here now, what did it matter? He allowed himself to be drawn towards a settle near the hearth, where a joint of beef was slowly turning on a spit. It was bitterly cold outside and the fire was warm, the smell of roasting meat enticing. Seth began to relax as he drank the rum Willie ordered.

"You made it then," he said, grinning.

"Aye, easy as robbin' the poor box after I left you, Captain. God, I never want to go through anythin' like that cliff descent again!"

Seth finished his drink and Willie winked at the serving wench. She replaced the empty tankard with a full one.

"Have you found us a ship, Willie?"

"Aye, that I have. There's a cargo to Marseilles and then we're off to the Gold Coast."

"Slaves?" Seth was beginning to feel much better. In a little he would have something to eat. It was some time since he'd eaten; keeping to the lonely roads and travelling at night he hadn't bothered with food. "I'm not sure I want that kind of a berth, Willie. I don't like the idea of one man making a slave of another."

"Chrissakes, Captain, they ain't men: they're animals. Good money in it, more than you'll get anyways else."

"Maybe I'd do better to slip across to France. I've got friends there. I could help them run contraband to England."

Willie stared at him as if he were

mad. "You'll hang. You're wanted twice over now."

"I've only killed one man," Seth said grimly. "I'll think about it, Willie."

"Please yourself, Captain." Willie grinned. "There's a wench over there givin' you a hot look. You must've caught her fancy."

Seth glanced distastefully in the direction Willie indicated. "No thanks, Willie. I'll stick to the rum."

"Fussy ain't yer?" Willie grinned. "Suit yerself, Captain. I'm gonna find myself a wench. This is my last night on shore; I intend to make the most of it!"

Seth nodded. He finished his drink and beckoned to the serving girl to bring him another. Perhaps if he drank enough he could blot out the look Arabella had given him before she ran away into the night. Somehow the memory of her face would not leave him. It made him feel guilty. He wondered what she was doing now and imagined her smiling into the face of the man she was going to marry, bewitching the poor devil just as she had bewitched him with her beautiful sea-green eyes.

Damn her to Hell! Would he never be free of her memory, of the sweet, fresh smell of her skin, the honey of her lips? Would she go on haunting him forever, spoiling him for any other woman? She was like a fever in his blood that came and went, growing stronger and stronger until it finally destroyed him.

He downed the tankard of rum in one go and ordered another, his black eyes leaping with pain and anger. Somehow he would get her out of his system if he bled to death in the attempt!

★ ★ ★

Arabella got out of the coach. It was old and smelt stale, but she hardly noticed. The guard gave her his hand, helping her down the steps. She gave him a faint smile. He was trying to be kind, but she was too weary to care. Sleep had become impossible: her dreams always turned to nightmares. It was easier to lie awake, staring at the ceiling with eyes which did not register what they saw, that way she could blot out the pain.

Philip had tried to help her, sitting beside her bed for hours while she refused to answer his patient questions. He had tried to keep the affair hushed up, but it was impossible: there had been too many witnesses. He had been forced to let the law take its course, especially since she refused to let a doctor examine her.

"You want him to say I'm mentally ill, Philip. You are wrong. I'm not insane. I knew what I was doing."

"But why, Arabella? If you have a good reason we could get the best lawyer and . . . "

Arabella had refused to answer, saying only that he must forget her and marry Charis. In the end Philip had gone away. She knew he would have stood by her if she'd told him the truth, but the scandal would cause such a sensation. If she pleaded guilty it would all be over quickly, and she still had some pride left. She would rather hang than tell everyone what Richard had done. Besides, she wanted to die.

The gates of Newgate clanged shut behind her. Arabella shivered as she was taken inside. Immediately the stench hit her, making her retch.

The turnkey was leering at her, she noticed uneasily. He had been paid for easement so that she should not be subjected to the indignity of wearing chains, and arrangements had been made for her to have a cell of her own. She was not to be thrown in the common side with the thieves and prostitutes. This much Philip had insisted on and she had accepted. She did not fear death, but the waiting would be hard enough to bear without being torn to shreds by the other prisoners.

The turnkey was telling her she could

have special food and wine sent in if she had money to pay for it. She nodded, finding the man's grin difficult to bear. She thought of the small knife concealed in the bodice of her gown; perhaps it would have been better to take her own life before she was brought to this place. And yet somehow she shrank from that, preferring to pretend that none of this was real.

* * *

Seth's head felt as though he'd been banging it against a brick wall. He opened his eyes, groaning; then he stiffened in sudden shock as a bucket of cold water was thrown in his face.

"So you've decided to join us at last then? Well, ain't that kind of you! Git your arse off that bunk or I'll kick it from here to kingdom-come!"

Seth blinked foolishly as a face swam into his blurred vision. He became aware that he was staring at a red-haired giant of a man he had never before seen in his life. He groaned again as he swung himself into a sitting position.

"Where the hell am I?"

The man grinned. "Hell's just where you are for the next twelve months or more, mate. This is the *Fateful* — and closer to Hell you won't get this side of the grave!"

"The *Fateful*?" Seth echoed, becoming aware of the rocking motion beneath him. "I was in the Fishy Tale."

"Well, you ain't now. Rotten Willie had you carried on board when you were out cold. Still, the pressmen would've got you if we hadn't; not that there's much difference between this stinking tub and His Majesty's bleedin' navy. You'll get flogged here if you don't jump to it just the same, still, the pay's better."

Seth grimaced. "That will teach me to mind where I get drunk in future. I had it in mind to join some friends in France."

"Rotten Willie said you was a

captain. I hope you know your way around a ship, mate, else you'll wish you was never born afore this voyage is out."

Seth grinned and stood up, matching the red-haired giant inch for inch. "You'll not find me lacking. Besides, it will take two like you to make me, how many more of you are there on board?"

The other man roared with laughter. "Just me, mate. They call me Red, don't know why. I reckon as you and me are gonna get along all right. Come on now — afore the Captain goes on the rampage. He's a right devil when he's mad."

Seth's eyes glittered.

"So am I," he said.

★ ★ ★

Arabella felt the sickness rising in her throat again. She leant over the bucket and vomited, wiping her mouth on the back of her hand. It was the second time she'd been sick that morning. The same thing having happened to her each day for the past week, Arabella was forced to face the truth. She was with child. But who was the father of that child: Seth or Richard? She was haunted by the fear that it might be Richard's seed she carried in her womb.

But perhaps it did not matter. Perhaps she would be dead before her child was born. Philip had told her when he visited that her trial was to take place in a matter of weeks. Her case had aroused so much public interest that it had been brought forward.

Philip had made one last appeal to her, pleading with her to tell him why she had shot Richard.

"You would not understand," she said tonelessly. "Why did you come here? You should think of yourself and Charis."

"But Bella . . . "

"Please go now, Philip."

Philip stared at her in an agony

of indecision. Should he tell her that Richard was still alive? Would it shock her out of her apathy to know he was well on the way to recovery, or simply make her imprisonment harder to bear? Richard must have done something terrible to make Arabella hate him enough to attempt murder. Sometimes he thought he knew but his suspicions were so horrible he was afraid to pursue them. And yet he must do something or Arabella might spend years in this place!

He sighed. "Is there anything you want, Bella?"

"I want you to promise me you will not come here again. You must marry Charis and forget me."

"I cannot promise that, Bella. If you will not try to save yourself, then I shall do what I can even if it makes you hate me, too."

Arabella smiled sadly. "I could never hate you, Philip. You are not like Richard." She shuddered.

"I'm glad he's dead. What I want

now is for it all to be over. I want peace, Philip. Is that too much to ask?"

"No, it isn't too much," Philip said quietly; then his pity turned to anger. "By God! I would give my life to know what Richard did to make you like this."

She turned her face away. "It's best you do not know," she said. "Please go now."

Philip had left her then and Arabella lay down, letting her mind empty itself so that she was not conscious of the prison stench or the moans issuing from the other cells. But now the certainty that she was with child was destroying her calm. If the new life burgeoning within her was Richard's, better it should die with her. But supposing it was Seth's child . . . ?

5

ARABELLA felt as if she were walking in a nightmare. It was four days since her trial and she still felt unable to cope with what had happened. She shuddered, remembering the jeers and insults of the crowd, and the eyes of the judge as he asked if she had anything to say in her own defence. She'd shaken her head, waiting in silence for him to pass sentence on her. Then, as a tense hush descended on the courtroom, a man's voice broke the silence.

"Stop! I must speak . . . "

Arabella had looked round wildly as she heard the voice, her face white as she gasped, "No, you're dead. I killed you . . . "

But the man forcing his way through the crowd had been no spectre. He came up to her and she saw the haunted expression in his eyes.

"I'll tell them, Bella," Richard said, speaking only to her. "I'll tell them why . . . "

"No," she whispered. "Think of Philip — think of Charis . . . "

Richard's face contorted with agony. "I have to speak . . . "

"If you do I shall kill myself. I mean it, Richard. I will speak for myself, but only if you remain silent."

She had lifted her head proudly then, looking into the cold eyes of the judge. "I shot my brother because he betrayed my lover to the Revenue officers . . . " She met Richard's eyes briefly. "And for no other reason — no other reason!"

She'd spoken defiantly, proudly, seeing defeat in Richard's eyes. She had waited calmly for her sentence, but had not been able to repress a shudder as the judge spoke.

"Miss Pennington, you stand convicted of maliciously wounding your brother, Richard Pennington, with intent to kill.

You admit this was done, not from self-defence or just cause, but because you desired revenge. Can you give me any reason why you should not pay the severest penalty this court can offer?"

"No, my lord." Arabella closed her eyes, her senses swimming. Then she raised her head to look at him. "For myself I ask nothing, but I would beg clemency for my child."

A ripple of shock and excitement went through the crowd at this new scandal.

"Silence! I will have order in this court."

The judge's roar brought an immediate hush to the packed benches as they waited breathlessly for sentence to be passed.

"The court finds you guilty of the charges brought against you. Had you succeeded in your evil intention I should have had no choice but to pass the severest penalty. However, I have decided to be lenient with you. You will be transported to the

American colonies, there to serve a period of seven years as a bond servant."

"No." Arabella swayed dizzily as she heard the judge's verdict. She had expected to die, wanted it once Seth's child was born. But to face a life of slavery in a strange country; it was a more terrible punishment than she could ever have imagined. "You cannot be so cruel. It is inhuman!"

The judge glared at her. "Take care, Miss Pennington, it is within my power to have you whipped." He waved at the turnkey. "Take the prisoner away — enough time has been spent on this case already."

Arabella felt her arm gripped roughly. She was almost dragged from the witness box. But even as she stumbled, Richard stepped forward to support her. She shook off his hand, her face haughty.

"Don't touch me."

"Bella, I'm sorry. Forgive me . . . "

Her eyes flashed with scorn. "I hate

you, Richard. I shall never forgive you. Never!"

Richard flinched as if she'd struck him. He stood back to let her pass, his face a mask of agony.

In the days that followed, Arabella had hoped Philip would visit her, letting herself believe he was appealing against her sentence. Richard was still alive, surely transportation was too harsh for what she had done! Against her will she had begun to feel again. She no longer wanted to die. She was going to have Seth's child. She longed to be free again, to breathe the sweet air of Sussex and walk through fields still wet with dew.

But Philip had not visited her, and Arabella could not know he was afraid to come. She would never hear from him that he had found Richard hanging from a beam in the stables. Poor, gentle Philip was so shocked and bewildered that he found himself unable to continue the fight for Arabella.

So Arabella was taken from her cell three days after her trial, believing Philip had abandoned her. In the cold grey light of the early hours she was herded with the other women in the courtyard as she waited for the chains to be fastened about her ankles; but more than the uncaring brutality of the turnkeys as they thrust her into one of the waiting wagons, she felt the hostility of the other women.

"Oho, look what we've got here then," one of them cried. "If it ain't her ladyship!"

Arabella looked at the fat, blowsy woman who had spoken, sensing the bitter resentment behind her words.

"Come down a bit now, ain't yer? Transportin' is too good for you, I reckon." She spat in Arabella's face. "Murderess!"

Arabella silently wiped the spittle from her face.

A thin girl with close-set eyes squeezed up to Arabella on the floor of the wagon. "Take no notice of Peg," she whispered. "She's only jealous."

"Jealous?" Arabella stared. "Why?"

"Cos your trial caused such a stir; she was only taken for stealin' a man's purse after she bedded him. Bet you never meant to kill him at all, did yer?" She stroked Arabella's arm. "Men are best dead, anyways."

Arabella shrugged off her hand. "I meant to kill him," she said coldly. "Please don't touch me."

Peg gave a cackle of mirthless laughter. "That's done for you, Lizzie." She eyed Arabella thoughtfully. "You've got spunk, I'll give you that."

Arabella stared straight ahead, not bothering to answer. It wasn't that she wanted to make an enemy of either woman, but she was desperately trying to recapture the calm which had been hers in the early days of her imprisonment. Her silence increased the resentment felt by the other women, who had already endured the worst Newgate had to offer. She was to become increasingly aware of their hostility during the journey.

That night both men and women prisoners were herded into a warehouse on the docks like so many cattle. Bread and water was shoved in after them; immediately a fight broke out as the convicts scrambled for food.

Arabella felt unable to join in the free-for-all, helping herself to water after the others had finished. There was no food left for her, but she was not hungry. She moved away, finding herself a place to sit where she could almost be alone.

"Are you hungry? You can have some of this if you like."

Arabella was startled. She shook her head, instinctively refusing the man's offer. "No, thank you."

He thrust the bread under her nose. "You'll need it before this journey's over."

Arabella turned away. She did not like the way he was looking at her, and she was becoming aware of the muffled sounds issuing from dark corners all around her, feeling her cheeks burn as she realised what was happening. The men, many of whom had not been near a woman for months, had lost no time in selecting their partners. Despite their chains, couples were entwined in a grotesque parody of love wherever they could find a space.

Arabella shuddered as the man sat down next to her. Beneath the grime of prison filth, his features were not displeasing, but she did not find him attractive. She jerked her head away as he attempted to stroke her hair.

"Don't touch me!"

"Come on — it may be a long time before we get a chance like this again."

"Find somebody else," Arabella hissed.

"I want you . . . " He gave a startled cry as something silver flashed in Arabella's hand. "What's that?"

"A knife. I'll use it if you touch me."

"I don't believe you," he said, his fingers curling around her wrist. "You bitch!" He let go as he felt something sharp score the back of his hand.

"Now go away," Arabella said, thankful she'd managed to conceal the knife throughout her stay in Newgate.

The man jerked to his feet, sucking at his hand. "I ought to break your neck!"

"Try it. I've killed once. I'll kill again if I have to."

The man swore loudly, but shuffled off to try his luck elsewhere. From then on Arabella was left to herself, but she was afraid to close her eyes all night in case he returned. She would turn the knife on herself if she had to! She was never going to let a man use her in that way again.

But if Arabella was reluctant to spread her legs for a man, most of the other women were only too willing. The sound of their cries of pleasure and the satisfied grunts of the men filled her with disgust. They were like animals!

Memories pressed in on her, filling her mind. Silent tears slid down her face as she wept for the first time since the night she had run from Seth with his bitter accusations ringing in her ears.

"Seth . . . Seth . . . " Her heart cried out to him wherever he was. "Don't hate me, Seth . . . "

But by the morning Arabella's tears had dried. She was pale and tired when they came to take her and the other convicts on board ship. A small crowd had gathered on the dockside. Some had come to jeer the prisoners, others to snatch a last farewell before a loved one disappeared — perhaps for ever.

Arabella searched the faces eagerly, hoping to see Philip. He was not there. She accepted it more calmly than she would have believed possible before last night. From now on she could rely only on herself. If she was to survive the voyage she would have to learn to defend herself. If she wanted to eat she must fight for her food as the others did.

As the sailors began to push the

women relentlessly towards the holds, Arabella made up her mind that she was going to fight. She would live and she would bear a healthy child.

And one day she would be free again!

* * *

Captain Jethro Travers watched from the bridge as the convicts came on board. They walked with a shuffling motion, hampered by the chains around their ankles. The chains were necessary, he supposed, but he would have them removed as soon as the ship was well out to sea.

Amongst the filthy wretches below were thieves, rogues and murderers, and the overcrowded prisons could not cope with them all. Some of the convicts would survive their term of servitude to make new lives for themselves, but many would die, either on the journey or because they were unused to the harsh conditions in the New World.

Captain Travers shrugged his shoulders, preparing to turn away. There was nothing he could do for them, except make sure that conditions on board were as healthy as he could make them. Many captains kept the convicts below decks for most of the voyage, a practice which led to loss of life. Loss of life meant loss of profits as no payment would be made for dead convicts. Fresh air and exercise daily, salt water to wash away the prison stench, these were just some of the privileges Jethro considered essential.

He always paid great attention to the quality of the food brought on board, and he had long arguments with the owners of the vessel, using his influence as a share holder to good effect. In ten years as his own master he had lost only a score of convicts. Few other captains could boast as much. However, the numbers of convicts being sent to the American colonies these days were steadily decreasing. Of late the magistrates were less inclined to provide the Americans with cheap labour; and if the dissension between Britain and America continued it could lead to war. If that happened Jethro was not certain where his loyalties lay.

He shrugged his shoulders. He doubted the colonists would be as easy to subdue as most Britons seemed to think but what could he do if His Majesty King George III was set on a blind confrontation with those stubborn men who had carved an embryo nation from a wilderness?

He was about to go below when his eyes chanced on a girl's face. She stood out from the filthy rabble below like a pure white lily. Her ankles were chained just as the others and her gown was stained, but she had obviously made an effort to keep herself clean.

As he looked at her, Arabella glanced up and their eyes met briefly. She appeared to look through him, and he was struck by the deep sadness in her lovely face.

★ ★ ★

The two women closed in on Arabella. They were out to teach 'Madam' a lesson, but neither of them dare face her alone. It was known she carried a knife and they were taking no chances.

The ship had been at sea several weeks now, and despite all the measures taken by Captain Travers, the holds stank unbearably. Already two women had died of fever and three of the children were sick. Arabella was suffering as much as the others, but they had never accepted her. Peg had hated her from the beginning, and Lizzie was nursing an unnatural passion for her which would never be returned.

Arabella eyed her attackers warily. In the past weeks she had learned to defend herself against the spiteful jibes and sly pinches, but this was the first time anyone had deliberately set out to attack her. She took her knife from the bodice of her gown, holding it ready.

Peg made a snarling sound deep in

her throat and sprang at Arabella, but she sidestepped. Then Peg grabbed a handful of Arabella's hair, howling with rage and pain as the knife blade scored her upper arm. Screaming like a wild thing, she clasped her fingers round the wound and retreated, leaving Lizzie to face Arabella alone. Suddenly Lizzie sprang, her fingers clawing at Arabella's face. Arabella put up her hands to defend herself and the little knife clattered to the floor, to be swooped on by one of the other women.

"Kill her, Lizzie. Kill the bitch!" Peg screamed.

Arabella went down under the clawing, spitting Lizzie. They rolled together on the floor in a frenzy of hate, biting and scratching like two wildcats.

Suddenly the hatch was wrenched open and a sailor appeared in the square of light above. "What's going on?" he demanded. "Why all the noise?"

Then he saw the two women still rolling on the floor together. He came down the narrow ladder, forcing his way through the crowd of women. He aimed a kick at Lizzie's belly, making her release her hold on Arabella. She jerked away, retching and writhing in agony.

"Who started it?" the sailor asked, and the fingers pointed at Arabella. "Right, the Captain will want to see you — and you."

Suddenly Peg darted forward clutching the little silver knife, blood still trickling from her arm.

"She had a knife; she just come at me for no reason."

"You can tell that to Captain Travers."

The sailor thrust Arabella up the ladder in front of him, grabbing Peg as she tried to hold back.

"I didn't do nothin'," she wailed.

"Git up there afore I kick your backside. You, too, skinny."

Lizzie struggled to her feet. She eyed him resentfully, her hatred of all men centring on him. She straightened up as she passed and spat in his face. He hit her across the mouth, twisting her arm cruelly as he forced her up the ladder.

On deck he looked at the three women, his mouth curving scornfully. "My, aren't we a pretty sight?"

Arabella raised her head. "You would look no better if you had been forced to live in the disgusting conditions in that hold."

"Oho, we've got a lady amongst us, have we?" The sailor leered at her. "The Captain is gonna love you!"

Arabella ignored his taunts, knowing he wanted her to fly at him in a rage so he could hit her as he had Lizzie.

Captain Travers was seated at his desk, a pile of papers scattered in front of him. He sighed as the knocking broke his concentration. "Come in."

"Fighting in the women's hold, sir."

Jethro looked up, frowning as he saw Arabella. The weeks below decks had taken away her appearance of freshness; her gown was stiff with salt where she had tried to wash out the stains, and her hair had a dull look, but the pride and arrogance were still there.

"Well, what happened?"

"The other women say this one started it, sir." The sailor indicated Arabella, laying the knife on the desk. "That's hers. She attacked this woman without provocation."

"That's right," Peg said quickly. "She meant to do fer me."

Jethro looked at Peg's arm, which had stopped bleeding. He picked up the knife, testing the point with his finger. It was sharp enough to inflict a painful wound, but the silver blade was too soft to make it a lethal weapon. He looked at Arabella. "Is this yours?"

"Yes, Captain."

"So you can speak. Are you ready to tell me what happened now?"

"I have nothing to say."

He tossed the knife onto the desk. "A pretty toy but hardly a murder weapon. Nevertheless, we shall not return it to you."

"What should I do with them, Captain?" The sailor looked at him.

"Take those two back to the hold. There will be no punishment this time — but any further lapses will result in a flogging." He glared at Peg.

"What about this one?" The sailor jerked his head at Arabella.

"You may leave her with me for the time being."

The sailor's face fell. There was clearly to be no flogging today. He thrust the other two women out of the cabin in front of him, causing Lizzie to stumble. He'd been looking forward to seeing Arabella humbled at the end of a lash!

Arabella stared at the floor. She could well imagine the captain's reason for singling her out, and the prospect of warming his bed for the rest of the voyage filled her with despair.

Captain Travers studied her face. Her features were very fine, and her complexion had been lovely before the salt water roughened her skin. With a little care she could soon be beautiful again.

"Would you like to tell me what happened now?" he asked.

"I have nothing to say — sir."

Travers grinned at the slight inflection on the last word. He pressed the tips of his fingers together, regarding her thoughtfully. It was seldom one of the convict women impressed him as she had from the beginning. He'd found himself watching her when she came up on deck with the other women, watching and admiring. It was not his habit to bed the women on his ship; he liked to keep business and pleasure strictly separate. But this woman was different.

"Would you like a bath?" he asked. "With fresh, warm water . . . "

The suggestion conjured up wonderful, tempting pictures in Arabella's mind. How long was it since she had been able to feel really clean? But the price was too high!

"I should prefer to go back to the

hold with the others."

Jethro frowned. "Why?"

Arabella clasped her hands in front of her, eyes downcast. "If I could just have the bath I should be very grateful, Captain."

"What makes you think I'm suggesting anything more?"

She looked at him then. "Aren't you?"

"And if I were, would that be so terrible?"

"Yes, for me it would." Arabella's eyes travelled over his heavy features and thickset body. "You are not unattractive, Captain Travers, but I would give the same answer to any man. The price you ask is too high."

"Why?" He fired the question at her. "You don't look as though you would hate men — What made you shoot your brother?"

"You know about me?"

"Yes." His eyes flickered over her face. "Why do you hate men?"

Arabella studied his face for a few

seconds. Somehow she sensed that he was a just man, there was a chance he would understand if she told him the truth.

"He raped me," she said in an emotionless voice. "He locked me in my room while he betrayed the man I loved, then he came to me again. He wanted to be my lover."

Jethro felt the sickness churning in his stomach. He had witnessed many forms of cruelty in his life and very little shocked him, but Arabella's calm statement made him want to vomit.

"Why didn't you tell the judge your story? No court in England would have convicted you if the truth were known."

Arabella smiled wearily. "I have very little left, Captain Travers, but I still have some pride."

"Pride? Aye, you have that, and guts." Jethro frowned. "We have passengers on board, a man and his wife, did you know that?"

Arabella shook her head, bewildered

by the change of subject.

"The woman has recently given birth to a child. Both she and the babe are sickly. They need someone to look after them, will your pride allow you to undertake the task, Miss Pennington?"

Arabella stared. "You mean not go back to the hold — nor stay with you?"

Jethro snorted. "If I were the man you think me, Miss Pennington, I should have you flogged and thrown into the sea for your insolence." He got up and crossed the cabin floor, pulling back a curtain to reveal a small recess. "During the day you will act as nurse to Mrs Jackson, at night you will sleep here, alone."

Arabella closed her eyes briefly. "You are very kind, Captain Travers. I wish there was some way — some other way I could thank you."

Jethro smiled wryly. "Perhaps you will change your mind before we reach Virginia, if not . . . " He shrugged carelessly. "Now — how about that bath?"

She gave him a watery smile. "I should like that very much, Captain. I didn't think men like you existed, except for Philip."

"Your lover?"

Arabella shook her head. "My eldest brother. He tried to help me, but in the end he abandoned me to my fate."

"You seem to have been unfortunate in your menfolk, Miss Pennington."

Bringing her eyes up to his, she was startled by the fierce desire burning there and backed away from him.

"You must not be afraid," he said. "I gave you my word. I shan't touch you — unless you give me permission."

He walked to the door, turning to smile at her. "I'll send water, and I think we might be able to find you a new dress."

"Thank you . . . " Arabella's throat constricted.

As the door closed behind him she began to weep.

★ ★ ★

Arabella bent to pick up Captain Traver's coat which had been thrown carelessly on the floor. She smiled, wondering how he usually managed to keep his quarters tidy: he was not the neatest of men.

She pressed her hand to her back as she straightened up; lately it had begun to ache a lot. Then she turned to find Jethro watching her, a thoughtful look in his eyes.

"How is Mrs Jackson?"

"A little better. She and the child are both sleeping, so I thought I would tidy your cabin."

"Thank you. We sailed without a cabin boy this voyage." His eyes narrowed as he looked at her. "You are having a child yourself, aren't you?"

"Yes."

"Who is the father, your lover or Richard?"

His abrupt question made her shudder. "I don't know."

"How will you ever know?"

"I shall know."

"And if it's Richard's?"

Arabella shook her head. She refused even to consider the possibility. It had to be Seth's child. The thought of Seth's child growing inside her was all she had.

Jethro ran his eyes over her questioningly. "When will it be born?"

Arabella knew she had conceived in November; it was now April. "In July," she said.

"Then your child will be born in Virginia. I expect to enter the Chesapeake Bay by mid-June."

"The Chesapeake Bay," Arabella echoed. "What is it really like?"

"The Chesapeake? It's like a grand reservoir served by countless tributaries, with great spears of land on either side. The first settlers named them Cape Henry, after the Prince of Wales, and Cape Charles. The land is rich and fertile; everything seems to grow bigger and faster than in England. It's a country of bright colours, still wild and untamed."

Arabella shivered. "Do the Indians still attack the white settlers? I've heard terrible stories about the way they massacre whole settlements."

Travers shrugged. "It has been better since the French wars ended, though they do sometimes attack isolated farms. I expect you know the story of Pocahontas and how she saved Captain Smith's life?"

"Didn't she lay her head on his and say that to kill him they must first strike her?"

He smiled. "So they say; anyway she continued to be friendly with the settlers and was baptised in the name of Rebecca. For a time there was peace, then the Indians decided they would drive the whitemen from their country for good, and they darn near succeeded! Fortunately, the settlers were warned and banded together. Since then the Indians have tended to melt away into the wilderness, but as more and more land is cleared there are bound to be clashes."

"You seem to know a great deal about the colony."

"I should do; my brother and I are partners in a small tobacco plantation. One day I'm going to give up the sea and retire there; meanwhile, Paul looks after my interests."

"Oh." Arabella was suddenly alert. "Then you must know the other planters; what are they like?"

He frowned. "You mean what will it be like as a bond servant? It depends on who buys your bond. Most of the men are decent enough, but even the best of them expect value for their money; you will be made to work hard."

"I don't mind work: surely I've proved that?" Arabella's chin went up.

"You'll find it harder in the fields, but perhaps you'll be lucky enough to go as a house servant. I shall do my best for you."

"You've done a great deal for me already. I wish I could repay you . . . " She took a deep breath. "I'm willing to try if you like."

Despite his promise, Jethro could not control his eagerness. He crossed the floor of the cabin in quick strides, folding his arms about her hungrily. But even as he did so, he felt the deep shudder of revulsion run through her and let her go.

"No, I won't force you."

Arabella blinked back her tears. "I'm sorry. I thought I could. I owe you so much . . . "

"You owe me nothing," he said angrily. Then he pushed past her and went out.

Arabella stared after him, knowing she could not blame him for his anger. She had really thought she could go through with it, but she hadn't been able to stop herself shivering when he touched her. Jethro had accepted her silent rejection: few men would have held back as he had. Why couldn't she love him when he'd been so good to her?

Arabella tried not to think of the man who would be her master in the

New World. Would she be expected to lie with him? It was hardly likely she would meet another Jethro Travers; and her hopes of becoming Sarah Jackson's servant permanently had faded when Mrs Jackson told her they had no money to purchase her bond. She shivered as she reflected on the future, knowing that whatever Fate had in store for her she must find the courage to bear it somehow.

She must bear it for the sake of the child she carried.

Seth's child . . . Oh, please God — let it be Seth's child . . .

6

THE waters of the Chesapeake were unbelievably blue. Arabella held her breath, spellbound by the incredible beauty all around her. Silvery fish broke the surface in a flash of iridescent colour, while overhead birds wheeled and circled in the sky. As the ship sailed further into the bay houses seemed to spring up out of the luxuriant vegetation, their presence almost an intrusion in the wild splendour. And above all else, in the distance, the mountains soared majestically to the heavens, clothed in a blue mist which swirled lazily about the ridges.

Gradually, Arabella became aware of people on the banks, and boats drawing away from the shore. She shivered despite the warm sun. The voyage was over: now the years of her servitude would begin.

The other convicts had been brought up on deck, and she knew that, like her, they must be straining for a sight of the men in the boats, uncertain and frightened. She straightened her shoulders, knowing she must join them. Her privileges were at an end. She moved away from the rails to join the other women.

"Where are you going?"

Arabella was startled by Jethro's sudden appearance "To stand with the other women."

"No!" He gave a hoarse cry, his fingers biting into her flesh as he turned her towards him. "You did not believe I would let you be sold like a slave?"

Arabella swayed dizzily. "But you must. You have to sell my bond: it's the law . . . "

"There's no law that says I can't sell you to myself."

"Oh, Jethro." Arabella choked. "You can't take me back to England with you . . . "

"I shall have to leave you with Paul and his wife while I arrange for the sale of my share of the ship; then I'll come back to you." He smiled as he saw her tears. "Don't cry, Arabella. We'll work it out somehow."

The tears slid helplessly down her cheeks. "I can't let you do this," she whispered. "You will regret it one day. Let me take my chances with the others, Jethro."

"It is already done. I signed the papers a week ago and had them witnessed. It is all legal. You are going to the plantation as maid to my brother's wife. Ellen is a decent woman; she and Paul will care for you while I'm away. And when I return we'll be married."

The small boats had reached the ship now, and the sound of loud voices made Arabella glance towards the newcomers. The first to board was a huge, bearded man with a deep scar above his left eye.

"Back again, Travers," he boomed.

"I hope you've brought some decent women this time, that last wench of mine only lived six months. She was half-dead before I bought her."

"And you gave her a push into Eternity," Jethro muttered, turning to nudge Arabella towards the hatches. "Wait in my cabin — unless you would rather go with him."

Arabella shivered. She knew he was not serious, but the big man with the loud voice terrified her. She glanced at the huddle of convict women and pitied whoever was chosen by him. Feeling guilty because she was so much luckier than the others, she went below.

★ ★ ★

It was suffocatingly hot. Arabella's clothes were sticking to her and her back had been aching for hours. Her child was coming soon now, she felt it instinctively.

Leaving her bed, she went to the window and looked out into the darkness. The moon was obscured by cloud but she could see the dark shapes of the trees and the outbuildings — and away in the distance, the slave cabins. It had come as a shock to her to learn that Jethro and his brother owned slaves.

"It's necessary," Jethro had said, as he helped her into the wagon which had come to meet them and was driven by a black slave. "We treat them well — besides, they are ignorant, childish people. They're not fit to be their own masters. Anyway, it's often the only labour available: the bond servants run away after a while, and no white man wants to work for a master when he can have his own land."

Arabella had not replied. She had come too close to being a slave herself to dismiss the idea lightly. The blacks might be simple people, as Jethro claimed, but she was sure they felt all the pain and indignity of slavery as much as the British men and women who had come out on the ship with her.

But she had not told Jethro how she felt. How could she after all he'd done for her? She was merely his bond servant, even though he did not choose to treat her as one.

Paul Travers had been waiting on the steps of the house to greet them. He was a year or so older than Jethro and slighter of build, but the resemblance was marked. Both had the same wiry hair and tanned skins of men who spent their lives working in all weathers.

"I'm sorry I couldn't get in to meet you," he said. "Ellen had one of her headaches." Paul looked at Arabella curiously. "I didn't know you were bringing company . . ."

Jethro grinned. "This is Miss Arabella Pennington my intended wife."

Paul's face split in an incredulous grin. "By all that's wonderful, Jethro!" He clapped his brother on the back, laughing loudly. His brows lifted slightly as he noted Arabella's condition. "You

211

are very welcome, Miss Pennington. I can hardly believe it . . . "

Arabella flushed, realising he believed she was carrying Jethro's child. "Thank you," she said softly. "I am very glad to be here."

Paul's face softened as he saw her tiredness. "Come in and rest. You must be worn out with all that bumping around in the wagon. I'll have someone take you up to Jethro's room."

"Arabella would prefer her own room for now." Jethro smiled at her. "Mitty will look after you. Mitty, where are you? I know you're there — I can smell you. Get yourself out here fast!"

A large, fat black woman sidled out of the shadows at the far end of the porch. To Arabella's surprise she did not seem in the least upset by Jethro's rudeness. She padded up to him on bare feet, throwing her arms around him and hugging him to her ample breasts.

"Now you jus' hush your mouth, Master Jethro honey. You gonna upset this pretty lil gal. Ah can see you done got yourself a real lady. What you bin doin', Master Jethro? No lady's gonna take you if'n she's in her right mind."

Arabella held her breath, fearing she would be punished for her insolence, but Jethro merely laughed, slapping her backside.

"You'll go too far one day, Mitty, then I shall have to beat you."

Mitty smiled, shaking her grizzled head at him. "Then who's gonna make them honey cakes the way you likes 'em? Ah got turkey roastin' on the spit, corn and black-eyed peas jus waitin' for you."

Jethro groaned, his mouth watering after weeks of ship's rations. "All right, I'll forgive you — now take Miss Arabella upstairs and look after her."

"It gonna be a pleasure lookin' after your lil gal." Mitty glanced at the bulge beneath Arabella's gown and grinned. "Never thought you had it in you, Master Jethro, must've bin somethin' you ate Ah guess." She smiled at Arabella. "Miss Bella honey, Ah knows jus' what you needs — a nice relaxin' bath and then Mitty to rub your pore achin' back."

Arabella went with her willingly, drawn by the warmth of her smile and the promise of a real bath. Soon she was lazing in a tub of sweet-smelling water while Mitty sponged her back and rubbed scented soap into her long hair. Afterwards, she lay on the bed, relishing the firm stroking of Mitty's strong hands.

"You feelin' better now, honey?"

"Wonderful." Arabella sighed contentedly. "I haven't felt this good in ages."

"Master Jethro never should have brought you out here in your condition."

Arabella rolled over onto her back, looking up into the old woman's face. "He had no choice, Mitty: I was a convict on his ship. I was sent out here to be a bond servant."

Mitty's expression did not alter.

"That so, Miss Bella? Well, you got yourself a good man. Master Jethro is 'bout the best they come round here."

"I know. He has been very kind to me. I am grateful to him." Arabella sighed deeply.

Mitty looked at her, her wise old eyes seeing more than Arabella guessed. "Men like Jethro don't need gratitude, honey. He needs someone to keep him warm nights. Bin lonely far too long. Needs a lot of lovin' a man like that."

"I know. I mean to be a good wife to him. I shall learn to cook and — well, you understand, Mitty."

Mitty stared at her hard. "Ah reckon you bin hurt bad sometime, Miss Bella. Ah knows how it feels. Ah wasn't always lucky enough to belong to Master Jethro. Ah guess maybe the same thing happened to me once or twice. You got to put it right out of your mind if'n you gonna be happy with your man."

Arabella smothered a sigh. "Perhaps I will be able to soon. Will you help me, Mitty? There's so much I need to learn."

"No need for you to work, honey. You jus make yourself look pretty for Master Jethro."

"But I want to repay him for his kindness."

Mitty grinned. "Only one way a man like that wants his woman to pay — jus' spread your legs wide enough, honey, and let him take his fill of you."

Arabella could not help laughing. It was impossible to take offence at Mitty, because she spoke with all the sincerity of a simple, loving nature.

"Do you think I shall ever be able to forget what happened?"

"Give it time, Miss Bella. Maybe if you talked it right out of you it would go away. If'n it don't, Ah'll make a charm for you — make you hot for Master Jethro."

Arabella shook her head. "No. No charms, Mitty."

Mitty chuckled. "You gonna feel better after your child is born. Now you have a good sleep before dinner."

After Mitty had gone, Arabella drifted into a light sleep. She woke refreshed to find she was not alone. A woman with thin, sallow features and mousey-brown hair was sitting beside the bed, watching her.

Arabella sat up. "I was so tired. Have you been here long? You must be Paul's wife. I'm Arabella." She smiled but her smile was not returned.

"So you're Jethro's bride-to-be." The woman's voice was slightly slurred and Arabella noticed the smell of lavender water on her breath. "It was a pity he did not marry you before he brought you here. I suppose you realise there will be a scandal."

Arabella flushed, not wanting to admit she had been a convict to this hard-eyed woman.

"A mistake I intend to rectify as soon as possible." Jethro stood in the open doorway. "Mitty was coming to call you, Arabella, so I saved her the journey."

"Thank you." Arabella smiled at him.

Jethro nodded. "Paul was asking for you, Ellen. I'll wait outside while you dress, Arabella, then I'll take you down."

Arabella smiled inwardly. She was in no danger of losing her way. Jethro was simply forcing Ellen to leave.

Ellen got up, giving him a malicious glance. She was retiring from the fray for the moment, but it was plain she had no intention of giving up the battle. She intended Arabella to know who was mistress here; and in the weeks which followed, she continued to needle Arabella whenever she got the chance.

Jethro had not told his sister-in-law that Arabella had been a convict, though she knew he had confided in Paul. The younger man had seemed embarrassed in her presence for a few days, but now he appeared to have got over it.

Jethro intended to remain in Virginia

until after Arabella's child was born. Meanwhile, he was busy finding a cargo for the return journey, and he was often away from the plantation.

Jethro had forbidden Arabella to go far from the house on her own, and she was too lazy to disobey him. Mitty spoiled her, fussing over her endlessly and making her rest.

Arabella had grown to like the black woman, and was comforted by the knowledge that Mitty would be there when her child was born.

"Don't you worry none, honey," she reassured Arabella. "Ah'm gonna look after you. You gonna be jus' fine."

Arabella had discovered that Mitty had her own little room at the rear of the kitchens.

"Master Jethro says Ah ain't a slave no more," she told Arabella proudly. "Ah tole him Ah don't want to be free ifn it means Ah got to leave him. He said Ah can stay here jus' the same — only Ah a free woman: jus' like you and Miss Ellen."

Arabella heard the pride in Mitty's voice and smiled. How little it had cost Jethro to make his faithful servant happy: and how much he had gained!

She wondered if he was exercising the same skill with her. She had the illusion of freedom, but he held the reins and could tighten them whenever he chose. So far he had treated her almost like a queen, but for how long would he go on being patient with her?

Soon after their arrival at the plantation he had gone off to Richmond in the wagon, returning with several parcels for her. She exclaimed in delight over the lengths of cambric, muslin and dimity.

"Mitty will help you with the sewing, but I did not think it worth buying silk at the moment."

Arabella looked down at herself and laughed. "This is just what I need: my gown was so hot. You will spoil me, Jethro."

"Unfortunately I'm not a rich man.

I can't give you the life you had in England."

Arabella flushed. "I don't want it. I'm very grateful for all you've done for me." She reached up to kiss his cheek.

For a moment Jethro hesitated, then pulled her close to him. He tipped her face towards him, brushing his lips lightly over hers. Arabella froze in his arms, and he let her go reluctantly.

"Not quite ready yet. Never mind, I think the thaw is on the way."

Arabella could not answer. She knew it was only a matter of time before his patience evaporated: then what was she going to do? Somehow she had to make herself welcome his love-making. She had to forget the horror of that night when Richard raped her so brutally. She had to put away her memories of Seth.

Arabella sighed. Somehow she had to accept that she had lost Seth, though a part of her cried out that it would rather die than live without him. She had a duty to her unborn child, and to herself. It was time she learned to live again, to think of the future. A future that would include Jethro.

It was the problem of Jethro and their relationship which had kept her wakeful tonight; that and her aching back. She longed for Mitty's soothing hands to ease away the pain. Suddenly she gasped, realising that the nagging ache had become something much worse.

Arabella bit her lip, breathing deeply. I must keep calm, she thought. I must go down and wake Mitty.

She moved towards the door, a little cry escaping her as the pain tore through her.

The door of the bedroom opened before she could touch it. Mitty smiled at her, her eyes gleaming whitely in the flare of the candle she carried.

Arabella gave a shaky laugh. "How did you know?"

The black woman rolled her eyes. "Ah knows everythin' goes on in this house, honey. Ah heard you callin' me in my head."

"You mean you read my mind?"
Arabella laughed again as Mitty held
the covers for her to slip back in bed.

"Ifn it ain't so, why Ah here?"

Arabella realised she had hurt Mitty's
feelings. "Because you are wise and
wonderful — and I love you."

Mitty smiled. "You can mock me,
honey, don't make no mind to me."

"But you are wise, and I do love
you."

Mitty shook her head at her. "You
gonna be Master Jethro's wife. Ain't
right for you to care none 'bout me."

"Mitty — you old fraud! You would
hate it if you thought I didn't care. Or
perhaps you don't really like me?"

Mitty frowned at her. "You jus' hush
your mouth, honey. You knows Ah jus'
loves you to death!"

"And I love you," Arabella replied
in dulcet tones, smothering a gasp as
the pain coursed through her.

Mitty patted Arabella's hand. "Don't
you fret now, Miss Bella. Don't need
to hold it in with me. You jus' scream

ifn you wants to."

Arabella held on to her hand. "Oh . . . it hurts. Mitty!"

Mitty smoothed the golden hair back from Arabella's damp forehead. "That's right, honey, you hang on to me. It gonna be over real soon . . . "

★ ★ ★

But it was not over as quickly as Mitty predicted. For the whole of the night and the best part of the next day Arabella was wracked with terrible pains. Mitty soothed her as best she could, wiping the sweat from Arabella's tortured body and bathing her forehead with scented water.

The day wore on, becoming unbearably hot. Arabella tossed restlessly on her bed, hardly conscious of where she was or what she did. Only the pain was with her constantly, tearing at her with merciless regularity.

Once Ellen came to the door of her room, watching with a triumphant smile curving her pale lips. It was obvious she enjoyed the sight of her rival's agony.

"Go away," Arabella muttered through clenched teeth. "Mitty, make her go away!"

"Take no notice, honey," Mitty soothed. "She's only jealous 'cos she ain't got no little ones of her own."

Ellen's eyes blazed with anger. "One day you'll go too far, and then Jethro won't protect you any more."

Mitty ignored her, rubbing Arabella's back as she lay on her side with her knees pulled up.

"Do you trust me, Miss Bella?"

Arabella gasped as the pain ripped through her, beads of sweat rolling off her forehead. "Of course. Why?"

"Ifn Ah make somethin' to help you, will you drink it?"

"One of your charms?" Arabella bit her lip, rolling on her back to look at her. "All right. I can't stand much more of this."

"Ah knows that, honey, else Ah

wouldn't do it. White folks don't mostly like black folks' medicine. You take it easy, Ah won't be long."

Arabella nodded, hardly hearing her. The pain was so terrible she scarcely knew where she was. She had not known it was possible to feel such pain and still go on living.

"Mitty, help me. Help me!" she screamed.

"Bella — Damnation! Bella . . . "

That was Jethro's voice. Arabella opened her eyes and saw him standing by her bedside. She tried to speak but her mouth moved without forming the words.

"Where is that damned woman? Mitty! Mitty, get your black arse up here!"

"Ah'se comin', Master Jethro. No need for you to get in such a state. You git outta here now."

"I'm not leaving while she's like this — What have you got there?"

"Jus' somethin' for Miss Bella. Ain't nothin' special."

Jethro glared at her, a tide of dark colour spreading up his thick neck. "If she dies from drinking that filth I'll make you wish you'd never been born!"

"Now stop that, Master Jethro. Miss Bella ain't gonna die."

"I'm warning you . . . "

A scream of agony from the bed interrupted their quarrel. Mitty thrust the cup she was holding into Jethro's hands. She bent over Arabella, stroking back the damp hair.

"You're doin' fine, honey; one more big push and it will all be over."

"Help me. Help me . . . " Arabella moaned. She screamed again as the emergence of the child's head split her apart. "Oh God! Oh God . . . "

"It's all right, Miss Bella. It's all over now. You ain't got nothin' to do but rest."

Mitty drew the baby, sticky with its mother's blood, from between Arabella's outspread thighs, expertly tying the cord in two places before she cut it.

"You've got a beautiful boy, Miss Bella."

Arabella opened her eyes. "Let me see," she whispered.

Mitty brought the child for her to look at. "Did you ever see such a big child? No wonder he nearly killed you gettin' him out, honey. Look at them eyes, black as night. Ah never saw eyes like that before."

Arabella gave a sigh of relief. "I have," she said. "We'll call him William — after my father."

She closed her eyes, feeling the exhaustion wash over her. Sleep was reaching out to claim her. She was no longer aware of Mitty hovering about her, making her clean and comfortable. She did not see Jethro glance at her son and then leave the room. Worn out with her long ordeal, she slept.

★ ★ ★

Arabella bent over her son's cot, lifting the thin netting. She saw he was sleeping peacefully, one tiny fist clenched tightly into a ball. Sighing, she resisted the temptation to pick him up and cuddle him. He was so beautiful she could have spent all day simply looking at him. Letting the veil fall back in place, she returned to her seat on the veranda and picked up her sewing.

Mitty came out onto the veranda, carrying a tray with a jug of cool fruit juices she had prepared to her own special recipe. Setting the tray on a table beside Arabella, she padded across the veranda to where William's cot stood in the shade.

"My, my, ain't he jus' the most beautiful child you ever did see, Miss Bella? Ah never did see a child grow the way he does."

Arabella smiled. "He is gorgeous, isn't he?"

Mitty nodded her agreement, coming to look at Arabella's work. "Where did you learn to do them fancy stitches?" She pointed a thick finger at the smocking on one of the tiny gowns.

Arabella laughed. "It was considered proper in England for young ladies to be able to embroider. I can draw and dance, too, but I have never cooked anything in my life."

"Ah tole you, ain't no need for you to work."

"But I want to be useful, Mitty."

"Plenty sewin' needs doin' round here. Miss Ellen never lifts a finger if she can help it, and Ah can't sew — leastways, not pretty like you."

"Can you find me some mending to do? I must find a way of showing Jethro how grateful I am."

"Tole you before, honey, only one way to do that. You over havin' that great chile now, Miss Bella. Why don't you give some of the lovin' you lavish on little William to Master Jethro?"

"I wish I could, Mitty. You have no idea how much I wish I could."

"You want me to help you? Ah can give you somethin' make you so hot for Master Jethro you forget 'bout what happen before."

"One of your charms? I don't think so . . . "

"And what are my two favourite women gossiping about?" Jethro came and sat next to Arabella. "How about some of your special julep for me, Mitty?"

"Ah done made that for Miss Bella, but Ah spects it won't harm you none."

She poured the fruit juice into a tall glass and handed it to him.

"Thanks, Mitty. Now git. I want to be alone with Arabella."

"Ah's goin'." Mitty glanced at Arabella. "You think 'bout what I tole you, honey."

Jethro frowned as she padded across the veranda and went into the house.

"What has that old witch been saying to you?"

"She thinks I should make more fuss of you."

Jethro nodded. "Ignore her." His eyes travelled over Arabella's slim body, lingering on the high full breast and neat hips. "You are beautiful, Arabella.

I wonder if you know how very much I want you."

Arabella saw the eager light in his eyes and bit her lip. "I think perhaps I do. I — I'm very fond of you, Jethro, and I appreciate all you've done for me."

He was silent for a moment, then: "I leave for England the day after tomorrow. I would like us to be married before I go."

Arabella sighed. "I think we should wait until . . . "

"I want you to be my wife for your sake. At the moment you are still a bond servant. If anything should happen to me . . . "

"Please don't!" Arabella cried. "I need you, Jethro."

"Then marry me. Marry me this afternoon."

Arabella stared at him. "But how — how can we?"

"There's a little church down river from here. The preacher has been converting a bunch of Indians. He has agreed to marry us."

Arabella looked into his eager eyes, her throat constricting. He had been so good to her and she had not been lying when she said she needed him. He was her only friend in a strange land. She would be a fool not to take what he was offering.

"All right — if you're sure it's what you want, Jethro."

He laughed, draining his glass and springing to his feet. "Go and put on your prettiest gown, Arabella. I'll tell Mitty to prepare something special for supper tonight. We'll have a party, the whole damn lot of us: fieldhands and all!"

Arabella smiled, catching some of his excitement. She reached out and caught his hands. "I'll be a good wife to you, Jethro. I promise."

He held her hands for a moment. "I know that," he said. "Now — go and get yourself all fancied up!"

★ ★ ★

Arabella leaned into the crook of her husband's arm, listening to the plaintive music issuing from the direction of the slave cabins.

Paul and Ellen had tactfully withdrawn, at Paul's insistence, leaving the newly-weds alone on the veranda. Jethro smiled down at Arabella, tracing the line of her white throat with the tip of his finger.

"You're not sorry you agreed, are you?"

"No." Arabella gave him a tremulous smile. "But you'll have to help me. Promise you won't be angry if I can't respond as you'd like at first."

Jethro's hand trembled on her bright hair. "Are you sure you're ready?"

"Yes. I want to be a complete woman again. But please don't be angry if I can't . . ."

"I promise. You know I love you."

Arabella withdrew from his embrace. "I'm going up to our room now. Give me a few minutes, then come up."

Jethro nodded. He watched her

disappear into the house, then left the veranda to take a last walk in the scented night air.

Upstairs in the bedroom she was now to share with her husband, Arabella fumbled with the fastenings of her gown. She was shaking so much she could hardly untie the strings of her bodice.

"Let me do that for you, honey."

Arabella felt no surprise as the black woman padded silently towards her. Mitty was carrying a glass of a dark, fragrant liquid. She held it out to Arabella, a half-smile on her thick lips.

"What is it?"

"Jus' somethin' to help you relax, honey."

Arabella hesitated, then took the glass and sipped the spicy drink. Liking the taste, she drank it all and gave the empty glass back to Mitty. The black woman nodded and smiled, untying the strings of Arabella's bodice and helping her into a flimsy nightgown.

Arabella ran her hand over the silken

robe. "This isn't mine. Where did you get it?"

"It's Miss Ellen's. She bought it a long time ago and never wore it. She won't miss it."

Arabella laughed. "You're shameless, do you know that?"

"Sure do, Miss Bella honey." She looked at the empty glass. "No need to tell Master Jethro 'bout this. You jus' relax and be happy."

Arabella giggled, feeling rather like a naughty child as she slipped between the cool sheets. She lay back, closing her eyes as Mitty went out. At least she had stopped shaking, and she was certainly feeling less tense. She tried not to think about what was going to happen. She wasn't in love with Jethro, but he'd been kind to her and she owed him so much.

She had an odd floating sensation, as though her body no longer belonged to her. She was not tired and yet she felt so relaxed; somewhere between waking and dreaming.

She was not sure how long had passed before she felt the bed move as Jethro slipped in beside her.

"Are you asleep?" he asked softly.

Arabella sighed. "No."

There was a pause, then Jethro's voice close to her ear. "Oh, Arabella, I love you so much. Let me love you, my darling, don't be afraid."

Arabella tried to say she was not afraid, but the words wouldn't come. She just sighed again, moving closer to him as he took her in his arms. It felt good, she thought dreamily, snuggling up to the warmth of his body, inhaling his masculine smell. The hairs on his chest tickled her face. She laughed softly, her arms going round him of their own volition.

"Arabella. Oh, my love," he moaned hoarsely. "I've waited so long to have you like this."

Arabella could feel him trembling. He seemed very disturbed but she could not think why. She was not able to think very clearly at all. Jethro was touching her now, his hands caressing every part of her body. It felt good. She pressed herself against him, feeling the heat of his flesh scorch her, her lips opening beneath his as he began to kiss her.

A soft moan escaped her parted lips; she arched her back to meet his urgent thrusting as the hot liquid desire suddenly flamed within her. Her whole being was throbbing with a fierce wanting that shocked her awake. All at once she was straining beneath him, her legs spread wide as every nerve in her quivering body begged him to possess her.

"Now. Take me now, Jethro," she pleaded, writhing in a frenzy of tormented desire.

Jethro was surprised by the fierceness of her response. She was a tigress, a pagan goddess before the altar of love. Her wild cries sent him mad with delight, releasing all the pent-up frustration of the past months. He thrust into her savagely, thrilling to her demanding response, all conscious thought lost in the warm nectar of her flesh. She seemed insatiable, still throbbing beneath him as he spilled himself inside her.

He rolled away from her panting and laughing. "And to think I waited all this time. My God! You're wonderful. I've never known a woman quite like you." There was no answer. He turned towards her. "Arabella?" He touched her lightly. She arched herself against him, moaning softly. "Arabella!"

Jethro leapt out of bed and lit a candle. He bent over her, holding the flame close to her face. She seemed to be looking at him, but she did not see him. She was still writhing and moaning, obviously in the grip of whatever foul drug she had taken.

"That blasted black witch!" he yelled. "What the hell has she done to you?"

Arabella's lips curved in a foolish smile. "Jethro — make me hot for Jethro . . . " she slurred. "Love me, Jethro."

"Like hell I will! I never wanted this. You hear me. I never wanted this!"

Jethro had never felt so angry in his life. A red mist was forming in his brain as the disappointment and rage fermented inside him. It had not been Arabella responding to his love-making but some evil drug Mitty had given her.

"I'll kill that damn black bitch!" he snarled. "I'll teach her to meddle in my affairs!"

Jethro shrugged on his breeches, his face a white mask of fury. He glanced at Arabella, relieved that she seemed to have slipped into a peaceful sleep at last.

"I'll talk to you in the morning," he muttered savagely.

Then he went to the narrow wooden chest in the corner. Lifting the lid, he took out a leather whip with a long curling thong. He stared at it for a moment, then slapped the handle against his hand.

"I'll kill that bitch," he muttered. "I'll kill her!"

* * *

Arabella awoke as the full heat of the midday sun touched her face. She opened her eyes, blinking in the brilliant light. Her head ached and her mouth felt dry. She groaned and ran her tongue over her lips.

"So you're awake at last!"

Jethro's cold voice from the doorway cut through her consciousness like a knife. She sat up in bed, holding the sheet against her naked breasts. She could see he was angry, angrier than she had ever seen him before.

"What's wrong, Jethro?"

He crossed the floor in quick strides, tearing the protecting sheet away. Arabella gasped, crossing her arms over her breasts in an attempt to hide from his hard stare.

"Why are you looking at me like that? What have I done?"

241

"You weren't so modest last night." Jethro flung her the gown she'd worn the previous day. "Put that on I've got something to show you!"

Arabella swung her legs out of bed and stood up. She began to dress while he watched her. Jethro was furious, that was obvious, but why? Her memories of the previous night were hazy, but she was sure she had responded to his advances: too well if she could trust her own memory. Her cheeks burned as she recalled the wanton abandonment of their loving.

She finished dressing, lifting her eyes to his proudly. "Are you angry with me because of last night?"

Jethro's hand snaked out, his fingers curling about her wrist. "You took something that black witch gave you, didn't you?"

"Yes. You're hurting me, Jethro."

For a moment the fury in his eyes was so murderous she thought he meant to strike her. Then he flung her away with a look of disgust.

"Why? Were you so terrified of me that you had to drug yourself? You were half out of your mind — like an animal."

Arabella flinched. "I didn't know. I can't remember . . . " She touched his arm. "I just thought it would help me to relax. It wasn't you I was frightened of, Jethro, it was my own memories."

His eyes flared with anger. "Don't ever do that to me again. Do you hear me? I want you, but not like that. Not like that ever again!"

"I promise." She tried to smile at him. "I shan't need to. It has all gone, Jethro — the hatred and the fear. I think it would have happened anyway once I was over the initial step. Perhaps it was wrong to drink that stuff but Mitty was only trying to help. She knew I wanted to please you."

Jethro's face hardened. "That damned interfering bitch! She won't make the same mistake again in a hurry."

Arabella's eyes widened in horror. "What have you done to her?"

243

"I've taught her a lesson she won't forget. God only knows what she might have done to you! You were out of your mind last night."

Arabella felt the sickness clawing at her stomach. "So you took it out on her. Your pride was hurt because I had insulted your manhood by taking one of Mitty's charms. Well, I was wrong. I admit it — it was a terrible thing to do. If I had guessed what would happen I wouldn't have touched it, but I don't blame Mitty. She's a child, Jethro, a simple, trusting child. She worships you. Don't you know that?"

Jethro glared at her. He turned away from her accusing eyes, crashing his fist against the wall.

"She got what was coming to her," he muttered thickly. "I warned her. I warned her . . ."

"Where is she?"

Jethro wouldn't look at her. "In her room. I was going to show you what you made me do . . ."

"I'll go down to her. Maybe I can help her."

Jethro swung round. "You're my wife. I won't have you waiting on a slave. I'll get a girl from the cabins to tend her." Arabella looked at him.

"I am your wife, Jethro, and your bond servant, so you own me twice over. But I'm going down to do what I can for Mitty. You can stop me if you use force, I know that. If you do I shall hate you."

He gave a strangled cry. "Don't hate me, Arabella. I love you so much. You were so wonderful in my arms last night that when I realised what she'd done to you I went crazy."

"I don't hate you, Jethro."

"Arabella, I'm sorry." He moved towards her as if to take her in his arms but she avoided him.

"Let me go, Jethro. Let me go to her."

"Yes."

The word was forced out of him but it was enough.

Arabella turned and walked out of the room, leaving him staring after her in despair.

Mitty was lying face downwards on her mattress. At first Arabella thought she was unconscious, but as she bent to examine the bloody lacerations on Mitty's back, the old woman raised her head to look at her. Her eyes were faintly reproachful as she said,

"What you want to go tellin' Master Jethro for, Miss Bella honey?"

At the familiar words of endearment Arabella's eyes filled with tears. "I didn't tell him — at least, I don't really remember. I can't recall much of last night at all, except that your charm worked. Jethro says I was out of my head."

Mitty made a choking sound. "Ah must've made it too strong: it shouldn't have done that to you."

"It doesn't matter now." Arabella stood up. "I'm going to get some water to clean up your back. Where will I find clean cloths and salves?"

Mitty shook her head. "You don't wanna do that, Miss Bella. You git Cissy — that lil gal helps me 'bout the house some days. She'll look after me."

"I'm going to look after you myself." Arabella's voice was gentle but firm. "And when you're better you can teach me to cook. Until then everyone is going to have to put up with my efforts. That should show them your true value if nothing else does!"

Mitty chuckled as she heard the note of satisfaction in Arabella's voice. She gave up the struggle, too weary to argue further and recognising the stubborn streak in her new mistress. Until now Arabella had been labouring under a burden of gratitude. Somehow Mitty sensed the change in her. She wondered if Master Jethro really knew what he'd taken on when he married Miss Bella. Master Jethro liked having his own way too much for his own good, and Miss Bella wasn't about to let him walk right over her. It looked as though there might be storms ahead.

Mitty wasn't bitter about the beating she'd received: the first since Jethro bought her. She had sensed the pain behind his rage. She was saddened by what had happened, but she understood him. And she loved him.

She looked at Arabella as she returned with water and clean linen.

"Don't you go blamin' Master Jethro for what he done. He a good man when he ain't mad, Miss Bella."

"I know. I don't like what he did to you, Mitty, but I think I understand. Now lie still while I fix your back." Arabella gave a smile of pure malice. "And then I think I'll make Jethro a meal — like a good wife should . . . "

7

ARABELLA watched as the black woman, Tassie, finished feeding William and laid him back in his cot while she fastened the bodice of her calico dress.

She grinned at Arabella. "He sure was hungry."

"Yes. I don't know what would have happened to him without you."

Arabella's smile was a little wistful: she had never really accepted her inability to feed her own child, but had been forced to admit the need for a wet-nurse when her milk proved insufficient for William's needs.

Tassie giggled shyly. "It's a pleasure, Miss Bella. You want me anymore now?"

"No, I'll see to William now. You go and help Mitty in the kitchen."

"Yes, Miss Bella."

Arabella bent over the cot as Tassie departed, smiling as her son gurgled up at her. At first she'd resented the need for Tassie to move into the house so she could suckle William whenever he was hungry, but now she had learned to be grateful. Without the black woman's rich milk her son might have died. To show her gratitude she had promoted Tassie to the kitchens instead of sending her back to the fields.

Ellen had complained bitterly at the change. She'd made a big issue of it one night at dinner.

"This isn't the governor's mansion, you know," she'd said. "We aren't rich folks. We need every pair of hands for the harvest as it is — Isn't that so, Paul?"

Paul swallowed a mouthful of fried chicken. "We can manage without Tassie. Arabella is right; it's too much to expect Mitty to do everything. Besides, Tassie is needed for William."

Ellen glared at him after darting a

look of hatred at Arabella. "Naturally *she* would be right."

"If it upsets you so much, Ellen, I'll send Tassie back to the fields," Arabella said with deceptive sweetness. "Of course that means I shall have to do all the cooking myself — and perhaps you could help with the sewing?"

Paul grinned but quickly hid his amusement. "Oh no, Arabella, I couldn't allow that. Ellen's health would never stand up to it. No, no, you keep Tassie. I'm sure Jethro would agree if he was here. After all, the plantation is more his than mine."

Ellen scowled, accepting the reminder in silence. As Jethro's wife Arabella was the true mistress of the house. For years Ellen had thought of the plantation as belonging solely to her and Paul. Jethro's infrequent visits scarcely bothered her, since they seldom lasted more than a few weeks; but soon he would be coming back for good and there was no doubt who would be in charge then.

Paul seemed glad his brother was going to help run the plantation, talking eagerly of the extra land they would be able to buy with the money from Jethro's share of the ship. But Ellen felt herself overshadowed by the lovely young girl Jethro had married, and was becoming increasingly jealous.

She pushed away her food hardly touched. "I have a headache. I shall go to my room."

"I'm sorry," Arabella said. "Shall I send Mitty up to you?"

"Thank you. I would rather be alone."

Ellen's eyes swept over her haughtily, refusing the offer of a truce between them.

"I'm sorry, Arabella," Paul said as the door closed behind her. "I don't know what's got into Ellen these days."

"I expect it's my fault." Arabella frowned. "I tried not to interfere but there was so much needed doing. And with Mitty ill . . . "

"I know." Paul's eyes were appreciative

as he looked at her. "Ellen never seemed to care much for making a home. Of course her health is to blame. All those headaches . . . "

"Yes. I expect they are the reason for her moods."

Arabella believed she knew the cause of Ellen's mysterious headaches, but she had no intention of embarrassing Paul by mentioning his wife's drinking. He must be aware that Ellen shut herself up in her room in the long, warm afternoons so that she could indulge her passion for strong drink. Despite her attempts to cover the smell of wine on her breath, it showed in her eyes and the bright spots of colour in her cheeks. Paul had enough worries just now without a reminder of Ellen's problem.

Unlike many of the big plantation owners he worked in the fields himself, directing the efforts of the slaves. He toiled long hours in all weathers, coming home late at night, tired out and grey-faced.

Arabella asked him why the slaves did not try to run away when he was not there to watch them. He had shrugged his shoulders, smiling wryly.

"Where would they go? They know they would be caught and punished. In any case they would probably starve in the wilderness or be captured by someone else. I treat them well; they are better off here than most places."

"Yes, I suppose so. Mitty stayed even though she is free."

Paul frowned. "Jethro never should have beaten her like that. I've never known him to do such a thing before."

Arabella blushed. She could not explain the cause of Jethro's violent outburst. She still blamed herself for what had happened.

Arabella knew Paul would be relieved when his brother returned. The last tobacco crop had not been as good as expected, and the money from Jethro's share of the ship would buy the extra land so badly needed. There was a good supply of water on the new land, water which could save the crops when it had been particularly hot and dry as it had last season.

Jethro had been gone five months now; with good luck and fair winds he might be back by late spring. She had missed him, she realised. Was it possible she was at last beginning to feel something more than gratitude for him?

Before he left for England she had smiled and kissed him, not wanting to part in anger.

"I pray you will have a safe journey, Jethro," she said. "Will you do something for me when you reach England?"

"Of course I will." He looked at her as she hesitated. "What is it, Arabella?"

"Will you visit Pennington Towers? Talk to my brothers and tell them we are married. Tell Philip I have a son, Jethro, and that I am well and happy."

He had smiled at her then. "Yes, I'll tell them."

"And, Jethro, tell — tell Richard I have forgiven him."

"If that's what you want."

She sighed. "It is. I realise now that so much of it was my own fault."

Jethro had left her then. She knew he did not really understand, how could he when there was so much she had not told him? But somehow the bitterness seemed to have drained out of her, leaving her with an aching sadness and regret for the love she had lost.

Since then the months had passed swiftly for Arabella. Mitty had been ill for some time, and even when she was on her feet again she seemed to have lost some of her old energy. She had grown used to seeing Arabella about the kitchen, and she began to teach her how to cook.

Arabella spent many happy hours replacing the curtains which were worn and fraying, and making new cushions. And she asked Tassie's man, Abner, to clear a patch of garden close by the veranda so that she could plant flower seeds ready for the spring.

He came each night after he had finished in the fields, working while Tassie idled on the veranda giggling and calling to him.

After his work was done the pair often slipped away together for a time, Tassie returning for William's feed. Arabella knew she ought to reprimand the girl for going off without permission, but she hadn't the heart. Tassie must miss her man since she had started sleeping in the main house.

Now, Arabella sighed as she laid her son back in his cot. It was time she went to the kitchens to make sure Tassie was helping Mitty with the work.

Paul came out on to the veranda.

"How would you like to go into Richmond with me — and Ellen?" he asked.

Arabella stared at him in delighted surprise.

Although he was always willing to

bring anything she wanted, it was the first time he had offered to take her with him.

"I would love it, Paul. When?"

"As soon as Ellen comes down. She wants to order some new clothes, and I thought it was time you had some, too."

"Oh, Paul, how thoughtful of you. I must go and ask Mitty to keep an eye on William for me. Wait for me!"

Paul smiled indulgently at her excitement. Jethro was a lucky man, he thought, comparing Arabella's radiant beauty with Ellen's pale, sulky face.

"I'll make sure Abner has the wagon ready," he called, his eyes following her as she fled to the kitchens.

He was laughing to himself as he went out of the front door, failing to notice the gleam of jealousy in Ellen's eyes as she came down the stairs.

★ ★ ★

It felt strange to be driving along a street again after so many months. Richmond was a pleasant little town and there were several fine buildings to be seen. Arabella thought it prettier than many English towns with all the trees, exotic shrubs and open spaces.

Paul stopped outside a small dressmaker's shop, helping Ellen and then Arabella down from the wagon.

"I'll meet you here at about four o'clock," he said. "If you get tired of looking at clothes you can take a stroll around the town."

"And where are you going?" Ellen asked sharply. "To the nearest whorehouse I suppose."

Paul's cheeks turned a dull red, but he held his temper in check. "No, Ellen, I am not going to a whorehouse. I shall order the provisions we need, then go the club to talk with the other planters. We shall discuss the price of tobacco and how much more we could get on the open market if the British parliament would ease the trade restrictions. Satisfied?"

"Oh, it was just a joke," Ellen replied.

Paul gave her a look of dislike, then smiled at Arabella. "Pick whatever you like, Arabella. Mrs Phipps will send her bill into me as she does for Ellen. "

"Thank you. I won't spend too much."

Arabella gave him a warm smile, gratitude mingling with sympathy. It was not the first time Ellen had made this kind of remark in front of her, implying that Paul sneaked down to the slave cabins to lie with the black girls. Arabella wondered at his patience, knowing he was mostly too worn out to do more than eat his supper before falling asleep in his chair at night.

Paul climbed back on the wagon, giving the reins a little flick. Arabella followed her sister-in-law into the shop.

Mrs Phipps had seen them arrive and was waiting for them. She ushered them through into the privacy of her comfortable fitting room, sending one of her girls for refreshments.

"This is Mrs Jethro Travers," Ellen said with a twist of her lips.

"I was so surprised to hear Captain Travers had married at last. Now I can see why!"

Mrs Phipps fluttered about Arabella smiling and cooing. She bustled about the room, bringing out a procession of rolls of rich cloth and all the latest fashion magazines to arrive from England and France. The magazines were all at least six months out of date, but the sketches of gowns were exciting to a girl who had worn the same stained gown for weeks.

Arabella smiled as she read a sparkling description of a pink and silver paduasoy gown in the *Tatler*.

Sighing, she put the fashionable sketches away and picked two serviceable gowns in dark colours with detachable linen collars. She shook her head when Mrs Phipps spread out a bale of sea-green silk for her.

"But it would match the colour of

your eyes, Mrs Travers. It must have been meant for you."

Ellen was busy selecting a similar quality silk in a dull green for herself. Remembering Paul's instructions to make certain Arabella bought several gowns, she put on a false smile.

"You must have it, Arabella. What will you wear when we entertain guests?"

Arabella was surprised. Visitors to the plantation had been few, and usually came only to enjoy a cooling drink and talk business with Paul on the veranda.

"Are we going to entertain?" she asked doubtfully.

"Of course. It hasn't been possible lately because of my health, but when Jethro gets back we shall have a dinner party."

Arabella allowed herself to be persuaded. The silk was lovely, and it was a long time since she'd worn a really elegant gown. She picked up a magazine she had earlier discarded, flicking the pages over swiftly to find the design she liked.

"Do you think you could manage this, Mrs Phipps?"

The sketch was of an evening gown with a plain, full skirt and a narrow-fitting bodice. The neckline was square and cut low across the bosom with a delicate edging of lace. The full sleeves ended just below the model's elbows with another lace frill, and the front panel was lightly ruched.

"Oh, Mrs Travers, I'm sure you could not have chosen better," Mrs Phipps cried. "With your tiny waist it will look ravishing!"

"It's a little plain for my taste," Ellen remarked. "But I suppose it will suit you. You had better order a cloak to go with it. You ought to have a shawl and some lace caps as well."

Arabella was surprised at Ellen's generosity, but she let herself be swayed. She really needed the new clothes and Ellen was ordering lavishly for herself. She seemed to have forgotten the poor harvest, or perhaps she did not care.

Mrs Phipps was careful never to mention cost. Ellen brushed Arabella's tentative enquiries aside, telling her not to bother about it as Paul always took care of such details. Arabella had no idea what they were spending but thought it must be a considerable amount and felt rather guilty.

They left the little shop at last after an hour of poring over sketches and materials. Arabella was wearing a new gown. Mrs Phipps had suddenly produced it, saying it was an order for another customer who would not now be needing it. Since it was a respectable fit, wanting only a few tucks at the waist, Arabella agreed to take it. It was a soft woollen material in a delicate shade of blue, and she knew it suited her. It felt marvellous to be wearing a pretty gown again, and her excitement was reflected in the glow of her lovely eyes.

Ellen was in a talkative mood.

Indicating a large building with white marble pillars either side of the imposing front door, she said: "That's the Planters Club. The men meet there to drink and talk business. Sometimes they play cards, and occasionally they hold parties for the wives. Usually, however, the men don't take kindly to ladies being admitted." She laughed harshly. "I think they use it as a refuge: to escape from us."

Arabella shrugged. "Perhaps they think we should be bored by all their business talk."

Ellen wasn't listening. Her cheeks had gone bright pink and she was staring fixedly at a man who had just come down the steps of the club. Without saying a word to Arabella, she sailed across the road to meet him.

"Why, I declare, if it isn't Mr Clinton. How delightful to see you again."

The man hesitated and then raised his hat a fraction.

"Mrs Paul Travers, I believe." He

looked beyond her to where Arabella was hesitating on the opposite side of the road. "Won't you introduce me to your companion, ma'am. I don't believe I have the honour of the lady's acquaintance."

Ellen hid her annoyance, beckoning impatiently to Arabella. "Mr Clinton, may I present my sister-in-law — Mrs Jethro Travers."

Arabella smiled and offered him her hand. He held it for a moment, then raised it to his lips and kissed it.

Arabella withdrew her hand, resisting the temptation to laugh. Mr Clinton was an exceptionally handsome man. He exuded a strong masculine appeal, and was, she thought, well aware of it. She was sure few women even tried to resist his smile.

"Mrs Travers, I am enchanted. I had no idea your husband's plantation concealed such a rare bloom. An orchid no less."

Arabella raised her eyebrows. "You flatter me too much. Perhaps an English rose would be nearer the truth."

"Ah, you are from England. Of course! I should have known. Only British women have such wonderful complexions. "

This time Arabella laughed. Mr Clinton was a little too charming and more than a little too sure of himself.

He sensed her indifference and his vanity was piqued. Turning to Ellen, he gave her a flashing smile. She wriggled and laughed, looking up at him coyly.

"You are coming to the little party I'm giving next Sunday I trust?"

Ellen squeaked with dismay. "But we haven't been invited!" she blurted out.

He looked shocked. "Not invited? But your invitation should have been delivered weeks ago. There must be some mistake. I shall speak to someone very severely about this. I suppose it is too late to invite you now?"

"Oh no!" Ellen was embarrassingly eager. "We should be delighted to come."

"You are too kind, ma'am." He

tipped his hat to her. "I shall look forward to meeting you again — and you, Mrs Travers." His eyes travelled boldly over Arabella's face and figure. "Please excuse me, ladies. I have some business to attend to."

He strolled off down the street and Ellen turned to Arabella excitedly.

"Matt Clinton is the richest planter in the district. He gives wonderful parties — at least, they say he does. This is the first time we've been invited." She looked at Arabella thoughtfully. "We had better return to Mrs Phipps and make sure our new gowns will be ready in time. And we must buy some slippers. You can hardly wear those!"

Arabella looked at her shoes ruefully. She had worn them ever since leaving England and they were badly scuffed.

"But we've spent so much already. Are you sure Paul won't be cross?"

"Nonsense!" Ellen scoffed. "We must make the right impression or we shall not be asked again. You have no idea how long I've been waiting for this invitation. Mr Clinton must have heard about the new land we're buying. We were not sufficiently important to attract his attention before."

Arabella had her own ideas about the impromptu invitation, but Ellen was glowing with pleasure and she had no wish to spoil things for her. She agreed to return to the dressmaker's and from there they went on to purchase new slippers for them both.

They were loaded with parcels and band-boxes when Paul returned to collect them. Arabella was anxious in case he was annoyed with them for spending so much money, but he only smiled.

"I can see you both enjoyed yourselves. Good."

"Paul, we've been invited to Matt Clinton's party next Sunday!" Ellen cried.

Paul's brows rose. "What brought that on? Or can I guess? I suppose he saw Arabella."

Ellen's sullen reply was lost on

Arabella. She was staring after a carriage which had just swept by, her face white and strained. Her heart was pumping so madly she felt she would faint. She stumbled as Paul helped her into the wagon.

He looked at her in concern. " Is something wrong?"

Arabella shook her head. "I think all the excitement has made me tired."

"I hope you aren't going to be ill with the party next week," Ellen snapped.

"No. I shall be all right in a moment."

Paul took up the reins, and Arabella was left to herself as the wagon trundled off. Her heart was racing so wildly that she hardly heard Ellen's stream of excited chatter. The man in the carriage which had just passed them had looked so much like Seth that for a moment she had believed it was him. Now she thought about it she realised there were several differences. The man was dressed in expensive clothes; his skin was very tanned and he had a dark moustache. Besides, how could it possibly have been Seth? She must have been mistaken. The likeness was remarkable but merely a coincidence.

As her pulse returned to normal she gave a little laugh. What difference could it make to her — even if the man had been Seth? Seth hated her.

Besides, she was Jethro's wife.

★ ★ ★

Arabella glanced at herself in the opulent gilt-framed mirror and smiled. The simplicity of her gown was at odds with the shameless luxury of the bedroom Matt Clinton had put at her disposal for the evening.

Arabella moved away from the mirror as Ellen came in. She was wearing a fussy gown of bronze silk with a surplus of frills, and clutching a string of amber beads.

"Aren't the rooms just too wonderful?"

271

she exclaimed. "I've never seen any-thing so beautiful in my life. And look — look what Mr Clinton sent me as a gift." She thrust the beads under Arabella's nose.

Arabella frowned. "They are lovely beads — but you're not going to accept them?"

Ellen looked annoyed. "Why not? He can afford it."

Before Arabella could reply a knock at the door diverted Ellen's attention. She opened it, staring at the ebony face of the slave standing there.

"Yes, what do you want?"

"Mr Clinton sent me, ma'am. I have something for Mrs Travers."

"I am Mrs Travers. Give it to me."

His face was impassive. "I was to deliver it personally to Mrs Jethro Travers, ma'am."

Arabella came to the door, taking in the situation at a glance as she saw the slim velvet box he was carrying.

"Mrs Jethro Travers?" he asked. "Mr Clinton would be honoured if you would wear his gift this evening."

Arabella made no attempt to take the box from him. "Please thank Mr Clinton, but tell him I must respectfully decline his generous offer."

For the first time there was a flicker of something in the servant's eyes. "As you wish, ma'am."

"But aren't you even going to look?" Ellen exclaimed as he turned away. "Don't you want to know what he sent you?"

Arabella picked up her shawl. "I have no intention of accepting his gift, so why bother to look?" She held the door for Ellen. "Shall we go down now?"

Ellen tossed her head. "Well, I intend to keep my necklace."

Arabella sighed, not wanting an argument. "If Paul doesn't mind, why should I? I have my own reasons for refusing Matt Clinton's gift. Shall we leave it at that?"

Ellen shrugged. "I hope he isn't offended."

Arabella smiled. "He will probably be amused."

Ellen looked puzzled, but Arabella did not explain. Matt Clinton's strategy in allowing her sister-in-law time to show off her own gift before sending Arabella's had not had the desired effect, but it was rather amusing. She wondered what his next move would be.

They went downstairs together, following the other guests towards the main reception rooms. In the first room long tables with sparkling white cloths were laid out with a lavish selection of exotic foods on huge silver dishes. And black slaves in fancy liveries were circling with trays of ice-cold champagne in crystal glasses.

Apart from the slaves it was a scene Arabella might have witnessed in an English drawing room. However, as she mingled with the other guests, listening to snatches of conversation, she discovered one distinct difference. Beneath the charm and the smiles was a hardness, a determination rarely found in English polite society. These were another breed of men. Men who had either left their own lands to start a new life in America or were descendants of the first pioneers who had clawed an existence from a savage wilderness. With their courage, sweat and blood they had made Virginia the prosperous State she was today; and they were fiercely proud of what they had done.

"You'd think those damned British would learn after the riots in Boston: the cargoes destroyed in the harbour must have been worth all of eighteen thousand pounds."

"And yet still they try to tax us. It will lead to war."

Overhearing the conversation between two planters, Arabella moved away. She felt a little out of place amongst all these hard-voiced Americans. She was not quite certain how she felt about the prospect of a war between the two countries. She supposed she was an American now, but she still felt like an Englishwoman. However, she was aware that the colonists had a valid complaint against the British government. The introduction of import taxes had annoyed the Americans; and though most of the taxes had now been lifted, the British government's stubborn refusal to lift the tax on tea had led to the riots in Boston and the dumping of several thousand pounds' worth of tea in the harbour.

The British had retaliated by blockading the harbour and pushing several bills through parliament which were meant to bring the New Englanders to their knees. Instead it had hardened the feeling against the mother country and given birth to a rash of smuggling up and down the coast.

Arabella had heard Paul talking about sending part of their crop out with one of the smugglers, and she knew that many of the goods they bought these days had never paid any kind of tax:

British or American. For a time the ladies of Virginia had refused to buy British goods, and some of them still insisted on wearing homespun as a protest.

The mood of the colonists was for separation; and men like Franklin in England, and Jefferson, Henry and Randolph in America, were steadily proceeding towards this end. And from what Arabella heard as she passed through the room, Matt Clinton and his friends were already beginning to make their own plans.

Ellen was dancing. Arabella refused an invitation to do the same, deciding to go out on the balcony for a little air.

It was cooler on the veranda. Arabella could smell the aromatic scent of tobacco burning, and she had a feeling she was not alone. She thought she could make out a dark shape in the shadows at the far end of the veranda, but as no one spoke she took no notice.

"I hope you are enjoying yourself, Mrs Travers?"

Matt Clinton's voice made her jump. She frowned as she realised he had followed her out on to the veranda.

"I think I should be hard to please if I were not, Mr Clinton."

"Call me Matt, please," he said, moving nearer to her. "Why aren't you dancing?"

"I wanted to be alone for a while."

"Why? You are far too lovely to waste your time looking at the stars alone."

Arabella sighed. "Are you asking me to dance?"

"Dancing holds as little appeal for me as it would seem to for you, Arabella. However, I can think of several ways we might spend our time more pleasantly. Perhaps you would like to see more of my house? I doubt if anyone would notice if we were to slip away for a while."

"Oh, I think they would, Mr

Clinton, and draw altogether the wrong conclusions."

He raised his brows. "Did you not like the pearls I sent you?"

Arabella's lips quivered. "Was it pearls you sent? I am not for sale, Mr Clinton, whatever the price."

"You have all the hallmarks of an aristocrat: what are you doing married to a man like Travers?" His hand moved caressingly up and down her bare arm. "I could give you so much, my dear, and your husband need never know a thing about it."

Arabella was no longer amused. She lifted her head proudly, her eyes flashing. "Nothing you could give me would change my mind. I was a convict on Jethro's ship. He bought my bond and then he married me, even though I was with child by another man. I have no intention of betraying his trust. Now, if you will excuse me, I shall join my husband's brother and his wife."

"Wait! If you think I'm going to let you go so easily you are mistaken."

Clinton made a grab at her but Arabella moved swiftly out of his way.

"If you try to touch me I shall scream. Now get out of my way! And try to behave like a gentleman."

"Bravo, Arabella, spoken like a true Englishwoman!"

A man moved towards them out of the shadows at the far end of the veranda. He spoke with an English accent; and even before the light from the ballroom windows fell across his face, Arabella knew him.

"Christopher!" she exclaimed.

Allingham laughed. "Why so surprised, Arabella? Did it never occur to you that I might be here? Or had you forgotten me completely?"

"Should I have remembered you?"

Allingham's brows rose. He turned to Matt Clinton. "Forgive me for interrupting, but I was forced to listen since there was no way of escape."

Clinton scowled. "Mrs Travers and I were having a private conversation."

"Which I think the lady had brought

to an end. A gentleman would allow her to leave now, Clinton."

Clinton's nostrils flared. "Are you suggesting . . . By God! I'll not take your insults lying down, Allingham. You will meet me for this."

"Whenever you wish."

"No!" Arabella glared at the two men. "I will not allow you to make me the subject of a scandal. I do not want or need your help, Mr Allingham, and I would prefer it if you left immediately."

Christopher's lips curled. "Obviously I was mistaken. My apologies, Clinton."

He left the veranda abruptly.

Clinton smiled. "Perhaps we can continue where we left off now, Arabella."

"My name is Mrs Jethro Travers." Arabella gave him an icy stare. "I am not interested in having an affair with you, but in case you are not convinced, you might like to know why I was a convict. I shot a man who raped me."

Arabella smiled as she heard his gasp

of astonishment, making her escape while he was still too stunned to stop her.

She went back into the lighted ballroom, watching the swirling skirts and the sparkle of costly jewels in the candlelight. Within moments she was accosted by a very young man who tentatively asked her to dance with him. She accepted with a smile. For the remainder of the evening she intended to make certain she was never alone.

From across the crowded room Arabella caught a brief glimpse of Christopher. He seemed to be arguing with a pretty but sullen-looking girl who wore a pink satin gown. He appeared to be urging her to leave and she was stubbornly refusing.

Arabella smiled to herself as she saw the frustration in his eyes. Apparently he had met his match. Julia was not quite the docile wife he had expected. Perhaps she believed her wealth gave her the right to dictate to him. Arabella wondered how he liked that . . .

Ellen could not stop talking about the party and all the marvels of Matt Clinton's house. It seemed to have made her even more dissatisfied with her life, and Paul was beginning to tire of her complaints.

He faced her across the breakfast table, sighing as he explained why they could not afford their own carriage.

"I've told you before, Ellen, we shall need every penny we've got for the new land. When Jethro gets back . . . "

"When Jethro gets back!" Ellen's face was a mask of discontent. "And just when is that going to be? He said he would be home by spring. It's spring now and he still hasn't arrived."

"Perhaps it took him longer to sell his share of the ship than he anticipated. Or perhaps he had bad weather. You know storms can add weeks to the length of a voyage. If the ship has run before the wind it could be blown miles off course."

Arabella looked anxiously at Paul. "You don't think something could have happened to him?"

Paul frowned. "Honestly, Arabella, I don't know. He's never been gone quite this long before."

For the first time Arabella faced the possibility of life without Jethro. She was still a bond servant within the strictest sense of the law despite being Jethro's wife. She could even be sold again. She was sure Paul would not be that inhuman, but Ellen would not want her in the house. Where could she go?

Paul saw the odd expression in her eyes. "Don't worry," he said smiling. "Jethro is too wicked to die young; he'll turn up when he's ready."

Arabella laughed. "Yes, I expect so."

Ellen looked from one to the other, glaring. She got up abruptly and went out.

★ ★ ★

Arabella was sitting on the veranda nursing her son and enjoying the first really warm day after the rainy season had finally dripped to an end. She smiled as William reached up and patted her face. He was eleven months old now and forward for his age, having taken his first tottering steps.

Mitty and Tassie spoiled him shamelessly, and Paul was almost as bad. He often came to join Arabella on the veranda while she was nursing her son, taking a break away from his work in the fields.

So when the horseman first came into view she thought it was probably Paul coming to enjoy a cooling drink as he sometimes did. But as the rider dismounted and walked towards her, she saw it was someone else. She stiffened as he approached, the smile of welcome freezing on her lips.

"Hello, Arabella."

"If you've come to see Paul, he is out in the fields."

Christopher grinned lazily. "You

know better than that. I came to see you. I have thought of you constantly since that night at Clinton's."

"Really? I haven't given you another thought." Her eyes glittered.

His mocking smile made her want to lash out at him. Did he still think she was a foolish child to be drawn into his net at will?

"I heard you mention your son the other night and it has been nagging at me ever since." Christopher looked at her eagerly. "Is the boy mine?"

Arabella's laugh was harsh. "I might have known. You wouldn't have bothered to ride all this way just to see me, would you? But a son of yours, now that would be different. What is the matter, can't Julia give you a child?"

His face tightened and she saw her shaft had gone home.

"She has had two miscarriages. I was a damned fool Arabella, I should have married you. There had never been another woman quite like you for me."

Arabella stared at him in disgust. He hadn't changed: he was still a selfish, ruthless brute who would take what he wanted from life no matter who he hurt on the way. He thought only of his desires, his needs. Julia's failure to have a child had evoked no pity from him, merely annoyance with her weakness. Suddenly Arabella felt sorry for the girl she had never met.

"You have no right to ask me a question like that, and I have no intention of answering it."

The eager glow left his face. "You hate me for what I did to you, and I don't blame you. What you did not know was that I was deeply in debt. I had to marry money, but I wanted you. I wanted you so badly I was prepared to go to any lengths to have you. After your father died I realised you meant more to me than I'd intended. I had to leave then or I would never have gone."

"But you went without a word to me, and you told Richard of our affair.

I could hate you for that betrayal alone, but I don't. You mean nothing to me."

"I suppose you are dazzled by Clinton's wealth," he sneered. "How convenient for you that your husband is away . . . "

"Was away." Jethro's angry voice startled them both. He came out on to the veranda, his face a mask of fury as he glared at Allingham.

"Jethro!" Arabella exclaimed. "When did you get back?"

"A few minutes ago. I came by the back roads. I wanted to surprise you," he said bitterly. "Well, aren't you going to introduce me to your friend?"

Arabella flushed, his anger stinging her. She wondered how much he had heard, and how much more he had read into Christopher's spiteful words.

"This is Mr Allingham. I knew him in England."

"Obviously, since there seems to be some question as to whether or not he is the father of your son. Well is William his?"

Arabella realised he would know if she lied. "No, he is not William's father."

Jethro's face looked like something carved out of granite. There was a dangerous glint in his eyes as he looked at Christopher. "I believe you have your answer. You had better leave now or I might forget my manners and take a horsewhip to you."

Christopher bristled at the insult. "I'm ready to meet you whenever you wish."

"Fancy yourself with a sword, do you? Or is it pistols? I wouldn't waste my time playing childish games with you. Get off my land before I throw you off."

Christopher snarled with rage, launching himself at Jethro. Within minutes the two men were locked in a vicious struggle, crashing against the wooden rails which gave way with a resounding crack under their combined weight. Then they were rolling in the dirt, slugging at each other in mindless fury.

"Stop it!" Arabella cried, snatching up her son and retreating to a safe distance. "Jethro, he isn't worth it!"

Jethro ignored her. Arriving in Virginia only last night, he had driven straight out to the plantation, eager to see his wife after months apart. Finding her alone on the veranda with a stranger had aroused his basic instincts. He'd lingered behind the window shades listening to their argument while the frustration and rage built inside him. Now he was getting it out of his system the only way he knew how.

It was an even contest, for though Christopher had the bigger build Jethro had all the hardness of years before the mast. Neither man lacked for courage or strength, but in the end it came down to stamina. After what seemed an eternity to Arabella, Christopher went down for the last time under the hammer of Jethro's fists. He lay there shaking his head and wiping the blood from his mouth.

Jethro stood swaying drunkenly on his feet, his battered face smeared with blood but his eyes triumphant.

"What were you saying about my wife and Matt Clinton?"

Christopher climbed to his feet. "It was mere jealousy. I was bitter and disappointed or I wouldn't have said it. If you'll take my advice you'll hang on to her for all you're worth. She's something special. I realised that too late."

Jethro clenched his fists. "I don't need your advice on how to handle my own wife."

Christopher nodded. He untied his horse and heaved himself into the saddle. Looking over his shoulder at Arabella, he managed a grin.

"I seem to have stirred up trouble for you again. I'm sorry."

Arabella's look froze him but she made no reply. She gave her son to Tassie who had come out with Mitty to watch the fight.

"Take care of William for me," she said. Then, looking at Mitty: "I'm sure you have work to do."

The two black women retreated hastily.

Arabella turned to Jethro. "Well, I suppose you are proud of yourself? What do you think I am — a bone for two dogs to fight over?"

Jethro took the kerchief from around his neck and wiped the blood from his nose. "What did you expect me to do — stand there and let him insult you?"

Arabella shook her head. "Oh no, you're not going to get away with that one. You believed him when he insinuated I was having an affair with Clinton, didn't you?"

Jethro shrugged. "I've been away more than nine months. Hell, Arabella! Clinton's a damned womaniser. He's a handsome devil too. After all, I wasn't the first with you, was I?"

Arabella sighed. She couldn't really

blame him for jumping to conclusions.

"No, you weren't the first, but I have not been with anyone while you were away. Do you believe me?"

"I guess so, but I'm not sorry for what happened. That arrogant bastard needed a whipping."

Arabella smiled. "It just so happens I agree with you."

He looked relieved. "Then you're not mad at me?"

"I'm far too glad to have you safely home to be angry for long. We were all worried about you, Jethro."

He reached out and drew her into his arms, holding her so that he could look into her face. "I've been hoping you would say that every league of the way home."

Arabella relaxed against him, lifting her face for his kiss. "I'm glad you're back," she said.

Jethro released her. "I went to see Philip."

"How is he?"

"He and his wife are both well.

Charis asked me to give you her love and tell you that if her child is a girl she intends to call her Arabella."

Arabella smiled. "Charis always knew what she wanted." She was silent for a moment, then: "Did you see Richard?"

Jethro took a deep breath. "He's dead, Arabella. He hung himself after your trial; that's why Philip couldn't come to you . . . "

Arabella's face went white. "Poor, poor Richard. How he must have suffered."

Jethro nodded grimly. "Perhaps. Philip was afraid to tell you, but I thought it best you should know."

"Thank you."

"Try to forget it, Arabella." He quickly changed the subject as he saw the pain in her eyes. "Philip was delighted when I told him we were married. He had all your clothes packed for me, and he sent your pearls and various other trinkets."

Arabella smiled. "The pearls were

my mother's. I left them behind when I was sent to prison. You have no idea how much it means to me to have them back!"

"The trunks are on the wagons. I'll have them taken up to our room."

Jethro smiled and touched her hair. "While I was away I tried to keep a picture of you in my mind, but the picture was never as lovely as you are right now. You won't ever leave me, will you?"

"Why should I leave you? Where would I go?" Arabella laughed up at him. "The sea must have addled your brain. Go on now while I find Mitty and make arrangements for your meal."

She walked away, glancing back over her shoulder to catch the odd expression in his eyes. She sighed; life was not going to be easy for them. Jethro loved her too much and he was a violent, jealous man. He wanted so much more than she could give him.

8

JETHRO awoke suddenly. Sliding his hand across the bed he found it cold and empty. He sighed, knowing Arabella would be in William's room where he had found her so many times this past year.

It was his fault they had quarrelled again. It was always his fault. He loved her so much, and yet the gnawing uncertainty would not leave him. Arabella never refused his love-making, but he felt she was holding back from him, that she did not really want him to touch her.

He was fiercely jealous of every man she looked at, including his brother. His jealousy had led to quarrels between them. He'd accused Paul of being in love with her, and he had not denied it. It would have been pointless when his love was there in his eyes every time he looked at her.

Jethro could not find it in his heart to blame his brother. Every day Arabella seemed to grow more lovely. She had blossomed in the climate of Virginia like a wild orchid reaching for the sky. The sun had kissed her skin to a warm honey, and her hair was like pale silk. She was everything he had ever wanted, everything he desired. And yet his jealousy was slowly destroying them both.

He had never imagined that one woman could mean so much to him. It made him angry.

Tonight they'd quarrelled over an invitation to one of Clinton's parties. At first Arabella said she didn't want to go, and he'd sneered at her, asking her if she was afraid of what he might discover. Then she said she would go and he accused her of hoping to meet Christopher Allingham again.

"He means nothing to me," Arabella said. "I wish I had never met him."

"But he was your lover. How many more were there, Arabella?"

"Does it matter? You knew there were others."

"If Allingham isn't William's father, who is? I want to know his name."

"What difference can it make?" She looked into his stubborn face and sighed. "His name is Seth Blackthorn."

"He's the one, isn't he? He's the one you can't forget. You still love him."

"I am your wife. I shall never see him again. Will you not try to forget?"

But he hadn't been able to forget, sniping at her until she lost her temper and yelled at him. He'd retaliated by hitting her across the mouth. He'd apologised at once and the quarrel ended when they made love. But the purely physical satisfaction was not enough for him. He wanted her love.

Now he threw back the covers, getting out of bed with sudden determination. There was something he had to do. He should have done it as soon as he returned from England, but he'd been afraid of losing her. He went out of the bedroom and along the passage to William's room.

She was sitting there just as he'd expected; her long hair a streak of silver in the moonlight. In her arms the child was sleeping peacefully.

Jethro wanted to kneel at her feet and beg her to love him but pride held him silent. As she turned to look at him, he said,

"Come back to bed, Arabella."

She laid the sleeping child in his cot and came to join him. "I heard him crying," she said when they were outside. "I think it must be his teeth again."

"Why didn't Tassie hear him?"

Arabella touched his arm as she heard the note of irritation in his voice. "I expect she has slipped out to Abner for a while."

"You're too easy with her," Jethro began, then laughed as he saw her look. "I suppppose you can't blame her."

They were back in their own room by

now. Arabella yawned and stretched.

"She is very good with William. He loves her. I'm sorry if I woke you, Jethro."

"It doesn't matter. No, don't go straight back to bed. I want to show you something."

He opened his sea-chest and took something from it. Then he lit a candle and handed her a folded sheet of thick paper.

"This belongs to you."

"What is it?" she asked, puzzled.

"A royal pardon, signed by His Majesty King George III. It's the reason I delayed my return. Philip begged me to wait until it finally came through."

"A pardon?" Arabella unfolded the document, staring at the fancy script in disbelief. She scanned it quickly and then read it again slowly before lifting her eyes to her husband's. "Jethro?"

"Richard wrote a letter before he died confessing his guilt. Lord Greenvale arranged an audience with the King for Philip and this was the result."

"But why didn't Philip tell me in the letter he sent?"

"I wanted to tell you myself."

"But you didn't tell me." She gazed up at him. "Why?"

His face tautened. "I was afraid you would leave me. You are free now, Arabella. Free to return to England if you wish."

Arabella looked at him sadly. "Why should I want to leave you?"

"To find the man you love: William's father."

"What point would there be in that? He does not love me. Besides, I'm your wife. My place is with you now."

"I'll let you go if it will make you happy."

Arabella knew how much it had cost him to make the offer.

"Thank you, Jethro," she whispered. "But I don't want to leave you. It is true that I still love Seth, and if I could turn back the clock and begin again I would do it. I cannot. Nor can I give you the love I gave to

301

him, but I do care for you. It is a different kind of love, but it is there in my heart if you will only accept it."

"My dearest love," Jethro choked. "If you had gone I do not know how I should have borne it, but I had to make the offer. I can't keep you against your will."

Arabella saw he was crying, and was humbled by his tears. A man like Jethro should not need to weep for his woman. She did not want to hurt him like this: it wasn't fair. She felt tears sting her own eyes as his arms went round her.

"Love me, Jethro," she whispered. "Make me forget there ever was another man. I want to forget."

She trembled in his arms, and he held her closer, sensing the change in her tonight. She was different somehow, as though he had set her free. Desire leapt within him as he slid his hand inside her nightgown, caressing her full, silken breasts. He felt her nipples harden beneath his searching fingers, and he groaned as she pressed herself against him. This was how he had dreamed of her so many times.

"Take me, Jethro," she urged him. "Love me now. I want you to love me."

Jethro moaned as the fire licked through him, making him throb with aching desire. He bent down to sweep her up in his arms.

★ ★ ★

"Clinton says there is sure to be war now. The British are fools, insisting on keeping that ridiculous import tax on tea even though the East India Company are losing money."

"They never learn," Jethro agreed with his brother. "You'd have thought that business in Boston would have taught them something, but they blunder on from one iniquitous bill to the next. I've seen the split coming for a long time. Well, maybe it's time we stood on our own."

"If there is going to be a war we'll need money for arms and ammunition. Clinton says we ought to start building our reserves now. He knows a man who is willing to take cargoes out right under the noses of the British, and he'll bring in arms or anything else we need."

Jethro whistled, raising his brows. "They'll hang him if they catch him. I wouldn't like to try it myself. Who is he?"

"He calls himself Captain Thorn, though there's some doubt if it's his real name. They say he left England in a big hurry. But you'll meet him at Clinton's if you go. He's really the reason for the party. There are still plenty of Tories left to go running to the Governor. We don't lack for traitors in Virginia."

Jethro grinned. "It depends which side you're on. Some would say we're the traitors."

"Traitors to a king who repeatedly sanctions bills designed to tax us unlawfully?"

"As I said, it depends on your point of view."

Paul frowned. "Well, are you with us then? Are you coming to Clinton's party? Thorn wants to meet you. He thinks you can help him with your knowledge of local waters."

"Why not?" Jethro asked, the memory of Arabella's warm mouth and silken body still fresh in his mind. He had the taste of her on his lips even yet. "I should like to meet this mysterious Captain Thorn: what harm can it do?"

★ ★ ★

Jethro glanced at Arabella, thinking how lovely she was. Her gown was of midnight blue satin; the bodice cut very narrow to accentuate her tiny waist and the ruched neckline plunged to an almost indecent depth, revealing an enticing glimpse of her breasts.

She held out her pearls to him. "Would you fasten these for me please, Jethro?"

He dropped a kiss on her shoulder. "You are beautiful tonight, Arabella."

She smiled at him. "Remember you chose the dress, Jethro, and if Clinton or any other man stares too much, for goodness sake keep your temper."

He laughed good-humouredly. "They can all look as long as they don't touch!"

"If anyone tries you will hear my scream from here to Lexington, so don't start imagining things every time a man asks me to dance."

He caressed her neck. "I love you."

"I know." She moved away as he tried to take her in his arms. "Later, Jethro: you will crush my gown."

He grinned. "It might be worth it. Maybe we won't bother with the party."

"I don't mind, Jethro. Parties like this are all the same."

"No, I'm looking forward to seeing

Clinton's face when he sees you in that dress. Besides, I want to prove I'm not jealous any more."

Arabella arched her brow. "Just don't fly at his throat the minute you see him, that's all I ask."

Jethro laughed. He took her arm, steering her out of the room towards the staircase. "Clinton must be fabulously rich, Arabella. But one day I'm going to get a house just like this for you."

"Not quite like this I hope. It's too flashy for my taste."

"I mean it, Arabella. With the new land we shall begin to make progress. Especially as I am here now to keep an eye on Paul's activities. I've already hired a new overseer and bought some more slaves."

She frowned. "What do you mean about Paul?"

"Oh, he had been creaming off a slice of the profits for himself each year." He smiled as he saw her shocked look. "The harvest is never quite as good as it promises to be somehow — and I dare say he finds other ways to cheat me a little."

Arabella was thoughtful. "Were my new clothes from Mrs Phipps deducted from your share of the profits?"

Jethro nodded. "Yes, plus a few of Ellen's I expect. I've known about his little perks for years, but I always thought he was entitled to the extra if he wanted it."

"But why cheat you? Why not ask for a larger share openly?"

Jethro shrugged. "I wish I knew. Let's forget it for now."

Arabella nodded. She was still thinking about what Jethro had told her when they reached the main salon. Why should Paul want to cheat his brother? What possible reason could he have?

As they entered the crowded room Clinton detached himself from a small group of men and came towards them.

"Mrs Travers, good-evening. I am delighted you could grace my little party this evening." His eyes bulged as he took in the daring cut of her gown and Arabella blushed. "Jethro, I declare your wife is the most ravishing creature!"

Jethro bared his teeth in what passed for a smile. He almost seemed to be willing Clinton to overstep the line, and Arabella realised why he had chosen the gown she was wearing. Nothing would please him more than to force Clinton into a fight.

Clinton looked at Arabella, then back at Jethro, a tide of dark colour creeping up his neck. He laughed nervously. "You must come and meet my special guest, Jethro."

"Ah yes, the mysterious Captain Thorn." Jethro smiled as he saw Arabella's raised brows. "I'm looking forward to meeting him."

But Arabella wasn't listening to him. Her eyes had been drawn across the room to the little group of men Clinton had indicated, and to one man in particular.

It was the man she had glimpsed briefly the day she had gone with

Ellen to order their new gowns. At the time she had convinced herself she was mistaken, now she knew there was no mistake. It was Seth! She recognised him immediately despite the changes three years had wrought. He looked confident, completely at home in a world he could never have entered in England.

Her first impulse was to run away before he noticed her, but she knew she dare not do it. She was feeling sick and dizzy, her heart thumping wildly as she followed the two men across the room. Her face was very pale and her hands shook so violently she was forced to hide them in the folds of her gown.

Then Seth saw her and his eyes narrowed to slits of black ice. A muscle began to twitch in the base of his throat and his lips went white.

She could only manage a half-smile and a slight movement of her lips as Clinton introduced them, saying:

"And this is the lovely Mrs Jethro Travers, gentlemen."

There was a murmur of greeting from the men; then Seth spoke, his voice cold. "Mrs Travers, I am honoured to meet you, ma'am." He stared through her as if she were a stranger. "Captain Travers, I have been hearing a great deal about you from these gentlemen."

"Really?" Jethro glanced at Arabella. "I hope it was all good."

"Yes, indeed." Seth ignored Arabella. "Perhaps we could have a private talk later? I am told no one knows these waters better than you. You may be able to help me — if you are willing?"

"Of course. If there is to be conflict between Britain and America, Captain Thorn, you need not doubt on which side you will find me."

"We shall talk later then."

Arabella felt as if she were suffocating. It was agony to be so close to Seth and yet not be able to say the things she longed to say. She was relieved to see Paul and Ellen enter the room.

Smiling brilliantly, she embraced the

whole group in her glance. "I know you gentlemen wish to talk business. If you will excuse me, I shall join my sister-in-law."

There were polite protests from most of the men, but she merely touched Jethro's arm lightly before turning away. The short walk to Ellen's side was one of the hardest things she had ever done in her life.

Paul smiled as she joined them. "You look lovely tonight, Arabella," he said.

"Thank you." Arabella's throat felt tight and there was a terrible roaring in her head. The world seemed to be spinning round her in a crazy kaleidoscope of purples and reds.

Paul noticed her pale face. "Are you all right?" he asked. "You don't seem well."

Hearing the concern in his voice, she tried to smile. "I feel a little faint. I expect it's the heat. Don't you find it warm, Ellen?"

"No. I don't feel it at all."

"Ellen is more used to our weather than you, Arabella." Paul looked at her. "Would you like to take a walk in the gardens?"

Arabella turned to him gratefully. "Would you mind? I think it might help to clear my head." She glanced at Ellen, sensing her antagonism. "I'm sorry to drag you away from the party. A few minutes outside is all I need."

"Oh, all right, let's go then," Ellen replied ungraciously.

Paul gallantly offered an arm to each lady, and the three of them went out onto the terraces.

The night air was cooler than the stuffy, crowded room, and scented with jasmine and honeysuckle. After a few minutes Arabella began to feel better. Paul was in a teasing mood, and went out of his way to lift her spirits, as though he sensed something had upset her. Gradually, the feeling of intense agony eased and she was able to breathe normally again.

"I'm fine now," she said at last.

"Shall we go back inside?"

As they returned to the house Arabella steeled herself against a further meeting with Seth. Neither he nor Jethro must guess what she was going through. However, on entering the salon, she saw the small group of gentlemen had dispersed. Seth was nowhere in sight. Arabella drew a sigh of relief as Jethro came towards them.

"I wondered where you had all got to," he said, frowning.

"Arabella was feeling the heat so we went outside for a breath of fresh air: all three of us."

Jethro looked at her anxiously. "Are you ill, Arabella?"

Arabella flushed. "Not exactly. I — I think there may be a good reason for my faintness just now. I didn't want to say anything too soon in case it was only a false alarm."

Jethro's look of delight made her ashamed of the small deceit. She was reasonably certain she was carrying his child, but she knew it was not the cause of her giddiness earlier.

"So that's why you didn't want to come this evening! Why didn't you tell me before?"

Paul was grinning at them both. "Well, this calls for a celebration! Jethro, you lucky devil! How did you manage it?"

Jethro looked stunned. "I have no idea. A father. I'm going to be a father!"

Arabella laughed huskily, a faint colour in her cheeks. "Well, don't tell the whole world about it."

"Why not? I want the world to know!" He took her hand, all doubts forgotten in his sudden surge of happiness. "Thank you, Arabella."

She smiled mistily, feeling the tears building behind her lashes. Jethro had been so good to her, but the affection she had for him paled beside the heat of her love for Seth. Seeing him tonight had rekindled that flame, bringing back all the memories she had tried so hard to banish.

Knowing he was here in Virginia would tear her hard-won peace to shreds. Even though he no longer cared for her she still loved him. Tonight had proved that if nothing else. The urge to reach out and touch him had been almost more than she could stand.

Why did he have to be here this evening? she thought miserably. Just when she was beginning to reach out towards a new life with Jethro. Why couldn't she put him out of her heart and mind? There must be a way. Somehow she had to learn to forget him!

★ ★ ★

It was terribly hot. Arabella's clothes were sticking to her back, and she could feel the trickle of sweat between her breasts. She went out onto the veranda, gazing at the heat haze hovering over the fields and wishing a cooling breeze would suddenly blow up.

William had been fretful all day, and

it was too hot to sit and nurse him. The heat seemed to have affected every member of the household. Ellen was lying in her room with the shades down and a jar of her favourite cherry wine; and even the slaves were suffering. Mitty had been grumbling to herself all day and Tassie had disappeared again.

Arabella sighed. Tassie was a problem. She had taken to slipping away whenever she felt like it, knowing her mistress had an ingrained dislike of inflicting punishment on the slaves.

It could not go on. Sooner or later Jethro would find out what was going on, and then there would be hell to pay unless Arabella could make Tassie behave sensibly. But brute force appeared to be all the black girl understood. She would smile and nod when Arabella asked her to do something, leaving the work untouched as soon as her mistress's back was turned.

Arabella knew Jethro had a similar

problem with the fieldhands, that was why he had hired Nat Paulus as the new overseer. He was a tough, sullen man. Arabella had disliked him on sight and she knew the slaves were terrified of him.

Jethro was pleased with the improvements the overseer had made, but since his arrival there had been a tense atmosphere which had not been there before. Despite their slavery the blacks had seemed happy enough until the last few weeks. Now everything had changed. Arabella had a terrible feeling that something evil was about to happen.

She tried to tell herself she was imagining it, because she herself was unhappy. Since the night of Clinton's party she had been having bad dreams, and often she woke up to find her cheeks wet with tears.

She knew Jethro was aware of her moods and that they made him angry, but the dreams haunted her. Always she saw Seth as if in a mist with a great chasm between them. He looked at her as though she were a stranger, his black eyes cold and distant.

"Love. You wouldn't know what love is."

The cruel words he had flung at her on that fateful night so many moons ago still haunted her. Oh, God, would she never forget them? Would she never be free of his memory?

If only she could forget. If she could be content with her life as it was. Jethro was a decent man and he loved her. She ought to be able to give him the love he deserved, but seeing Seth again had shattered the illusion of happiness she had begun to build for herself.

She was startled out of her reverie as Jethro came striding out onto the veranda, his face as black as thunder. Her heart began to beat wildly.

"What is it, Jethro? What's wrong?"

"Abner and Tassie have run, the damned fools! Paul and Nat have gone after them with the dogs."

Arabella stared at him in dismay. It

was her fault. She had been too easy with Tassie, and that had given the girl time to dream of freedom.

"You — you won't have them whipped, Jethro. Please, not Tassie!"

Jethro frowned, hating the necessity for what he must do, knowing it would cause trouble between them. "It's that damned wench's fault. I agree with Nat that Abner hasn't the brains to think of running. Don't look at me like that Arabella. I don't want to do it. I have no choice."

Arabella looked at him reproachfully. "There's always a choice, Jethro. Send her back to the fields if you must punish her. Please don't whip her: remember how you felt after you beat Mitty."

"That was different . . . "

The mournful baying of the dogs from the direction of the slave cabins made them look at each other. Jethro's face hardened, his lips becoming a thin white line.

"The dogs must have found them

already. The stupid fools! They should have known we would catch them."

"That's just it, don't you see, Jethro? They are children; naughty, thoughtless children. They would never have dreamed of running away before Nat came: he frightens them."

Jethro stared at her, torn between his convictions and a desire to please her.

"I have to make an example of them," he said at last.

"Please, Jethro, not Tassie." She caught at his arm. "Please!"

His face was taut. "I'm not a cruel man, Arabella. I'm not going to enjoy this, believe me."

She looked at him pleadingly. "Please don't do this," she begged. "I have a bad feeling about it, Jethro. I am asking you not to do it — for my sake."

"For your sake, Arabella? If I thought I meant anything to you I might let it go, but you don't want me." Pain flickered in his eyes. "What happened that night at Clinton's? Just who is the mysterious Captain Thorn, or do I know already? No, I won't let you turn me into a weakling begging at your feet for the favour of a smile. The slaves are my business."

"Jethro . . . " Arabella hesitated as she saw the look in his eyes. "I'm sorry. I didn't want to hurt you."

Jethro sighed. "We'll talk about this later. I've things to do right now."

He walked away. She stood with her head bent, covering her face as the sobs tore through her. What had she done to him — to them both?

She could still hear the dogs barking excitedly, and now a child's terrified scream. Nat would be enjoying this, she thought bitterly, not even the innocent children would be spared the spectacle. Arabella was sickened as she remembered the brutal floggings she had witnessed on board ship, and the deep lacerations on Mitty's back after she'd been beaten.

It was cruel and inhuman! She couldn't bear the thought of it happening all over again. Besides, it was partly her fault. If she had been stricter with Tassie at the start, the girl would never have encouraged Abner to run.

Arabella suddenly ran from the veranda, round the side of the house towards the cluster of the slave cabins. She couldn't let this happen, not to Tassie! Tassie had suckled William; without the black girl's milk her son might not have lived. Arabella was gripped by an unreasoning panic, a nagging fear that if she let this whipping go on something evil would result from it.

She was panting when she reached the slave cabins. She halted at the edge of the compound, staring in horror at the scene which met her eyes. Nat had lost no time in bringing the prisoners in. Abner had his ankles and wrists bound, and a rope was attached to a collar around his throat so that he could be dragged behind the overseer's horse like a dog. His face was cut and bleeding, and there was a huge gash in his right leg.

The other slaves were huddled together in a little semi-circle, watching something. Arabella's stomach turned as she saw Tassie being lashed to a whipping post with cruel leather thongs which cut into her flesh. She was moaning and weeping, almost fainting in her terror.

Even as Arabella watched, Jethro unfurled his long whip, drawing back his arm for the first blow. It cut through Tassie's flesh like a knife through butter, bringing a scream of agony from her.

Tassie's scream had an instant effect on Arabella. She ran to Jethro and threw herself at him, hanging on to his arm and preventing him from striking again.

"No, Jethro. You mustn't hit her again!"

Jethro's eyes flashed with fury. "Get back to the house. I warned you not to interfere."

"I won't let you do it. I won't!"

Arabella hung on to the whip, winding the leather thongs around her fingers and tugging at it. Jethro held on to it stubbornly, jerking it hard so that the thin leather cut into her flesh. She gasped with pain as it was torn from her grasp; then she flung herself at Jethro again and was thrust away so violently that she stumbled and fell in the dirt.

She lay stunned and shaken as the whip sang out again; but even while Tassie screamed, a dark shape moved swiftly from the huddle of slaves. Arabella heard a guttural snarl as the black body hurtled at Jethro; saw a flash of silver in the sunlight as a knife carved through the air, embedding itself in Jethro's chest. She screamed, watching in horror as he sank to his knees. Then everything was pandemonium.

A shot rang out and the slave slumped to the ground. In a daze Arabella saw that the man was one of those recently purchased from the slavers, newly brought from Africa, still raw and unbroken. Before any of the others could think of following his example, Nat turned his gun on them, daring them to move. But they were stunned and terrified.

Then Arabella was kneeling beside Jethro. She caught him as he swayed and fell against her, lowering him gently to the ground. She bent over him, tears running down her cheeks.

"Oh, Jethro, forgive me. I only wanted to stop you. You were destroying yourself, too, don't you see that?"

His eyes flickered open. "Not your fault . . . I was wrong . . . "

"Don't try to talk," she said, choking on her tears.

"We'll get you back to the house."

"No . . . leave me . . . nothing you can do." He smiled at her in his old way. "I loved you too much. Find him, Bella, find William's . . . " A trickle of blood ran from the corner of his mouth. He gave a little jerk and went limp in her arms.

"Oh no! Jethro, don't die. Please don't die. I'm sorry . . . "

Paul leant over her, lifting her gently

to her feet. "He's dead, Arabella. Let me have him now."

Taking Jethro's limp body in his arms, Paul began to walk towards the house, staggering under the weight. He refused Nat's help brusquely, his face grim.

Arabella followed behind. She was vaguely aware of Mitty close by. The black woman's wailing was a recrimination, a bitter reminder of what she had done.

In the slave compound they were cutting Tassie down, and carrying away the dead man. Two deaths in the space of a few seconds, Arabella thought hysterically. Two deaths because she had questioned Jethro's authority in front of the slaves.

Arabella was conscious of a nagging ache in her back. Something had happened inside her when she fell. She was losing her child. Later she would feel the tearing agony, but for now she was too numbed with her grief and guilt to recognise the physical pain.

★ ★ ★

Arabella felt the stab of Ellen's eyes as she walked into the dining room. It was the first time she had come down to dinner since Jethro was killed. The first time since she had miscarried his child. She had recovered from the miscarriage now but the torment lingered on despite the nights she had spent weeping alone.

"I'm surprised you dare show your face — you murderess!"

Ellen's attack was not unexpected. Twice she had come to Arabella's room while she lay wracked with pain, screaming abuse at her and sobbing wildly until Paul dragged her away.

Arabella wondered at her own blindness. Ellen's hatred for her had been obvious from the start. Ellen had married the wrong brother. She had wanted Jethro but either he had rejected her love or she had discovered her mistake too late. This was most likely the reason for her drinking and the quarrels with Paul. And Paul had known it, Arabella realised. It explained so much that had puzzled her.

She paused in the doorway, looking at Ellen sadly. "I am sorry. I shouldn't have come. I'll get something from the kitchen and take it up to my room."

Paul stood up and walked round the table, taking Arabella by the hand and leading her to her chair. "You will sit with us. It wasn't your fault."

Arabella sat down because she felt too weak to resist the pressure of his hands on her shoulders. She looked up at him, begging forgiveness with her eyes and finding sympathy in his.

"I'm sorry, so sorry," she whispered. "I never meant it to happen. I only wanted to save Tassie: and Jethro, from himself."

"I know," he said. "I begged him not to whip her myself. I've never needed to whip a slave before. It was Nat's fault they ran, not yours. He threatened to sell Abner if he did not work harder."

"Why did Jethro have to do it?"

Paul looked awkward. "He hasn't been himself for weeks. I don't really know why . . . "

"I do!" Ellen's voice was like the crack of a whip. "It was because of her — because she was tearing him apart." She got up, pushing her chair back with a clatter. "While she is at this table I shall not eat with you. It's your choice, Paul. But you will never be free. You will never be able to marry your little whore!"

Ellen turned and stalked out of the room.

Paul's skin turned a dull red. "I don't know what has got into her. I'm sorry."

"Please don't apologise, Paul. I was wrong to come down this evening, but I wanted to ask for your understanding and your forgiveness."

"I never blamed you, Arabella. I love you, just as Jethro did. He didn't blame you either."

Arabella choked back a sob. "Oh,

Paul, what have I done to you all? Jethro was so good to me and I destroyed him."

"He brought it all on himself."

"No. You only know a part of it. It was me. What I did to him." She looked at him steadily. "I shall go back to England as soon as I can get a passage."

"But this is your home. Jethro's share of the plantation belongs to you now."

"No. It is yours, Paul. I could not stay here even if Ellen did not hate me."

"If your mind is made up at least let me pay for your passage and give you something to live on until you are settled. I know Jethro would want that."

"Thank you." Arabella smiled mistily. "I shall miss you. You've been good to me too."

"What will you do, marry again? If I were free . . . "

"No, Paul. I doubt if I shall

marry — and if I did it would not be to you. Please don't waste your life in useless regret."

"I can't promise that, Arabella." His grin reminded her of Jethro, twisting her heart with pain. "But I know when a woman means no. I suppose you wouldn't kiss me — just once?"

"If you wish."

Arabella sat still as he came to her and bent his head. He drew her up into his arms, holding her against him for a moment. Then he let her go as he felt her lack of response.

He smiled ruefully. "Well, I asked for that. Jethro always had all the luck."

Arabella felt the tears rush to her eyes. "If only you knew," she whispered. "Oh, Paul, if only you knew . . ."

Then she turned and ran from the room, leaving him staring after her.

★ ★ ★

The waters of the Chesapeake were rippling with little white crests as the *Susanah Yorke* rode at anchor in the bay. Overhead the sky was grey and thick with cloud, a stiff breeze tugging at Arabella's cloak as she stood in the stern with Paul.

"I still wish you would change your mind and come back with me."

"No, Paul. I must go."

A warning bell gave the signal for all those not making the voyage to return to the boats. Paul squeezed her hand, his eyes regretful.

"Goodbye, Arabella. I don't suppose you will ever come back to visit us?"

"There is nothing for me here, Paul."

He nodded, accepting it at last.

Arabella watched as the rowing boats began to pull towards the shore, lifting her hand to wave to Paul. The British ship had weighed anchor: she was on her way home. But what was there for her in England? Despite her pardon she would still be an outcast, a fallen woman.

Paul had given her five hundred pounds in gold besides paying for her passage. It was enough for her to start a small dressmaker's establishment, she supposed. She had always had a flair for style; she could probably make a living for herself and William.

She smiled wryly as she saw herself as another Mrs Phipps, eternally smiling at the wealthy ladies who patronised her shop. But what else was there for her?

She turned away, deciding to go below. William was sleeping in the cabin and she wanted to make sure he was safe. Besides, she did not want to watch the shores of Virginia receding. Her grief and guilt would remain with her for a long time, but now she must look to her own future. She was still in her early twenties; a young woman eager for life, and yet she felt she had already lived a lifetime. She had made so many mistakes, mistakes for which she had paid dearly.

Was she to go on paying for the rest of her life? Would she never know the joy of loving again? Would she never be free of the memories which haunted her, the desperate longing for a man who had ceased to care whether she lived or died?

Her heart yearned for him. Where was Seth now? Oh, God, was she never to see him again?

9

FROM the bridge of the *Fateful* Seth could see the ship on the horizon through his long spy-glass. If his information was correct, the vessel was British, six days out from the Chesapeake and carrying documents which must never reach England.

It was the first time he had planned to attack a British vessel, though he had taken Dutch and French ships many times since he became the *Fateful's* captain; preferring to earn his living by piracy and smuggling to running slaves.

He sometimes wondered about the bizarre quirk of fate which had made him the *Fateful's* captain. During the first months of that nightmare voyage to the Gold Coast, Seth had accepted the beatings and cruelties he witnessed, enduring the hardships of his lot without complaint. He had known hard masters before in his years at sea, but never one who took such delight in the sufferings of his crew.

The outward journey had been bad enough, but the return voyage was doomed from the outset. Captain Jacks stripped the ship to the bare essentials in his determination to cram as many wretched slaves into the holds as possible. The *Fateful* lay heavy in the water, overloaded and stinking with the acrid stench of human sweat and excrement from the packed holds.

Seth knew he would never forget that smell as long as he lived. The weather had been unbearably hot for a month after they took on the cargo of human misery, and the slaves died like flies in the fetid holds. Then the ship was becalmed for a week, and the fever began to spread to the crew.

The tension had led to fights amongst the men; retribution following fast in the form of savage beatings. The men grumbled constantly, resentful and angry but too scared to do much about it.

Seth had remained an impartial observer for as long as he could. However, when Captain Jacks ordered Rotten Willie to be keel-hauled for making a foolish mistake, Seth's patience finally snapped. Before his friend could be murdered, he forced his way to the bridge, demanding the order be rescinded. Captain Jacks refused, his eyes bulging with fury as he glared at the man who had dared to question his authority. He had tried to strike Seth with a small cane he carried, but found his wrist gripped by fingers of steel.

Despite his cries for help not one of the crew came to his assistance. Seth had begged him to listen to reason but he had acted like a madman, suddenly producing a loaded pistol. In the ensuing fight Seth had killed him.

Afterwards he had given the crew two alternatives: to put him in irons and take him back to England or to sail with him under their own colours, knowing they would be outcasts without a country.

Most of the men had no homes and few prospects. The idea of becoming pirates appealed to them, especially as they were already carrying a lucrative cargo of black slaves.

Seth had been wise enough not to try and stop the sale of the slaves, though he had done what he could to ease their suffering for the remainder of the voyage.

However, he had refused to return to the Gold Coast for another cargo. Instead he persuaded his crew that it was easier to attack rich merchant ships and steal their cargoes.

So Seth became Captain Thorn, a pirate and an outcast. But now he had a country again, for another quirk of fate had led him to Matt Clinton at a time when Britain and the American colonies were on the brink of war.

Clinton and some of the other planters had been preparing secretly for months, and Seth had chosen to join them. It amused him to take out cargoes of tobacco under the very noses of the British and to bring in goods the colonists wanted without payment of tax.

However, attacking a British ship was a different thing. He reminded himself that this was war. If the two countries were not yet actually at war it could only be a matter of time. A congress was taking place even now in Philadelphia, and twelve of the thirteen colonies were forming the beginnings of a new constitution. Besides, he considered himself an American. The papers carried on board the *Susanah Yorke* could be vital to his adopted country.

He looked at the ship through his spy-glass again. This time she was close enough for him to pick out her name. She was the *Susanah Yorke* all right! His feeling of elation faded as he caught sight of a woman's gown. He swore loudly and shut the glass with a snap. Passengers or not the attack must go on!

★ ★ ★

Arabella was on the bridge of the *Susanah Yorke* when the *Fateful* was seen to be bearing down on them. Captain Smith had taken her under his wing, his sympathy aroused by her widow's weeds and her pale face. He was determined to make the voyage as pleasant as possible for her and to show his crew that she was under his personal protection, hence the invitation to the bridge.

Absorbed in his fascinating companion, he took little notice of the approaching vessel until she closed in on them. From her lines and the cut of her jib she appeared to be British but she was flying no flag. Then, just as he became aware of danger, the skull and crossbones was run up and a warning shot ripped across his starboard bow.

He was taken by surprise. The

buccaneers had once plagued the seas hereabouts, but the last fifty-odd years had seen vast reductions in their numbers. A few privateers still sailed with letters-of-marque, attacking any ship they considered fair game, but he had not heard of any British ships being attacked recently.

However, there was little Captain Smith could have done in any case. The *Susanah Yorke* was a merchantman not a warship and loaded down with a cargo of tobacco. Besides, he was carrying several passengers, families loyal to the Crown who found the political climate of the colonies too hot for their taste just now. Far better to let the pirates take the cargo than risk so many lives in an attempt to fight them off. Even while he debated the best course to take with the pirates, the *Fateful* had closed in and grappling irons were thrown across the side securing the two ships.

Turning to Arabella, he advised her to go below at once. But as she obeyed him he called her back, whispering something to her.

She nodded. "Yes, of course I will, Captain."

Arabella could hear shouting as the pirates swarmed aboard, and a loud voice demanding the surrender of the ship. She caught sight of some fighting from the corner of her eye as she went below decks, then she heard Captain Smith order his men to cease resisting.

Once below decks she went first to her own cabin. William had been fast asleep when she left him to go up on deck for a breath of fresh air. She did not want him to wake and be frightened by the noise. God only knew what might happen to them all if the captain could not appease the pirates!

William was still sleeping peacefully, his thumb in his mouth. He murmured fretfully as she picked him up but did not wake. About to leave, she remembered her mother's pearls. Balancing the child on one arm, she rummaged in her trunk and slipped

343

the necklace into the bodice of her gown. Then, recalling her promise to Captain Smith, she started out for his stateroom.

Her progress was hindered by terrified passengers who all seemed to be hurrying in the opposite direction. Some of them appeared to think the ship was sinking and a woman was screaming wildly. In their panic they rushed towards the upper decks and were sent back by the sailors who had orders to keep them below. The resulting confusion only increased the bewildered passengers' fears and led to scuffles.

Reaching Captain Smith's cabin at last, Arabella closed the door behind her. She laid her son on the bed while she hunted for the small chest the captain had asked her to destroy. He had said it was hidden in a recess to the left of the table where his charts were spread out. She found the charts and then the recess. Drawing back a curtain, she removed a pile of books and more charts, discovering the little chest at the back.

She picked it up and started towards the open porthole when the door of the cabin was flung wide and a huge, bearded man appeared in the doorway. Arabella ran towards the porthole, trying to thrust the chest through it; but before she could do so her wrist was imprisoned in a grip of iron.

"And what do we have here, my pretty?" he asked, grinning.

Arabella felt the chest torn from her grasp. It was thrown to another man who had followed the first into the cabin.

"Take care of that, Willie. I've no doubt it's what the Captain wants. I caught this wench trying to get rid of it."

Rotten Willie sniggered. "You'd better bring her along, Red. The Captain may want to see her."

Arabella shrank back as Red moved purposefully towards her. "No, I was only doing as Captain Smith asked."

Red's hand curled about her wrist again. "Willie's right, our captain will want to see you."

"Then let me bring my son." Arabella glanced towards the sleeping child. "I shan't try to run away."

Red nodded, releasing her. "All right, bring him but no tricks now!"

Arabella picked up her son, holding him to her as the big man pushed her ahead of him out of the cabin. She was trembling as she retraced her steps through the narrow gangways; on all sides she could see the pirates ransacking the ship. The other passengers were being forced to yield anything of value despite loud protests, and on deck the cargo of tobacco was already being brought up from the holds.

Arabella found herself pushed towards the bridge. A tall man was busy directing the pirate crew. His back was turned to her, yet she felt there was something familiar in the set of his shoulders. Her heart began to beat faster as he swung round at their approach.

"Arabella!"

"Seth . . . " she whispered. "You?"

"I found this woman trying to dispose of a small chest in Captain Smith's cabin, sir. I believe it contains what we were looking for, but I have men searching his quarters to make sure," Red said.

Seth nodded, recovering from the shock of seeing Arabella. "Did you ask this lady to dispose of certain papers, sir?"

Captain Smith glared at him. "So that's what you were really after — and you an Englishman. Traitor! I'll see you hang for this."

Seth smiled. "Aye, I dare say you will if I'm caught. However, I'm an American now and this is an act of war."

"We are not at war with the colonies, sir, despite the disgraceful behaviour of the citizens of Boston. You are merely a pirate seeking to hide behind your country's imagined grievances."

"You may be right. I am not prepared to argue politics with you. However, if war comes those papers would prove damaging. Names, dates, places: they must have taken your spies a long time to collect. And since you were so anxious to dispose of them, perhaps information of which we were not aware."

Captain Smith scowled. "What about my cargo and the passengers' valuables?"

"Spoils of war I'm afraid. My men must have something for their trouble." Seth smiled coldly, "At least you will escape with your lives."

Captain Smith glanced at Arabella. "Please ask your man to release Mrs Travers."

Seth's face became hard. "I'm afraid we must take the lady with us."

"But she is an Englishwoman — you cannot abduct her!"

"I have no choice, since, as you must realise, Mrs Travers knows my true identity. I cannot allow her to go on with you to England. Red, take her to my cabin please."

"Aye, aye, sir."

Arabella clutched William to her, shaking with suppressed fury. Her eyes flashed green fire at Seth. How dare he insinuate she would betray him to his enemies? It was the same thing all over again, but this time she would not run away in tears!

"Please don't be anxious about me, Captain Smith," she said with quiet dignity. Then, giving Seth a look of cold disdain: "Would you be good enough to have your men transfer my trunk to your ship, sir?"

Seth looked through her. "As you wish, Mrs Travers. Please go with my men now."

Lifting her head proudly, Arabella allowed herself to be escorted to the ship's side. One of the pirates took William from her while the red-haired giant swung her up in his arms and scrambled over the rigging, depositing her safely on the *Fateful's* deck.

"If you will come with me, ma'am," he said, and she was surprised at the respect in his voice. "I will take you to Captain Thorn's cabin."

She followed him obediently and was shown into Seth's stateroom; the door slamming ominously behind her. William had woken now and was staring at her with his big black eyes which were so like his father's. She cradled him to her, crooning softly.

"It's all right, my darling. There is nothing to be frightened of. Mama is here."

"Mama," he said, beginning to struggle in her arms.

She smiled and sat down, spreading his blanket on the floor for him to crawl at her feet. She watched him fondly, wondering what would happen when Seth saw him properly. Would he know William was his son? Would he care either way? She made up her mind that she would not tell him unless he guessed the truth for himself.

She was not frightened at finding

herself a prisoner on board the pirate ship. Her fear had vanished as soon as she saw Seth. She had no idea what he meant to do with her, but she doubted he would harm her. Perhaps he would take her back to the Chesapeake, even so they must spend several days in each other's company.

Arabella admitted to herself that the idea excited her despite the anger his coldness had aroused in her earlier. He despised her; he had shown that clearly when they met at Clinton's party, but for a brief moment that morning she had seen something very different in his eyes. It had faded quickly, to be replaced by the cold stare she dreaded so much, but it had been there. Was it possible that he still felt desire for her even if he no longer loved her?

Arabella heard shouting and the tread of many feet on the deck above. The pirates were returning to their own ship, and now the grappling hooks were being removed from the *Susanah Yorke*. They were moving. She went to the porthole and looked out, watching as they gradually drew away from the British ship. She watched until the *Susanah Yorke* was a tiny dot on the horizon, then she felt William tug at her long skirts. She bent down to pick him up, going back to her chair.

Soon now Seth would come to the cabin, and then she would learn what plans he had in mind for her. If he asked her to stay with him, if there was the slightest chance he still wanted her, she would do whatever he asked of her. No matter how angry he made her or how much he hurt her she knew she would go on loving him as long as she lived. But she would not beg for his love. She would not use William to secure a future for herself. Seth had rejected her love once, if he wanted it now he must ask for it.

★ ★ ★

Seth became aware of Red's curious stare. He sighed and shrugged, knowing it had been bound to come. One of the first rules he had ever made as captain was that no women were to be brought on board from captured ships.

"Well," he said, glaring at Red, "say it then."

"Say what?" Red tried to look innocent and failed, his lips quivering beneath the thick beard.

"Ask me why I broke my own rule."

"I thought it was because she knows your real name — you mean it wasn't just that, Captain?"

"Damn you, Red!" Seth growled. "I suppose you think you're being clever?"

Red threw back his head and laughed. "I always wondered who Arabella was; you talked about her a lot the night Rotten Willie had you carried on board. I've a good memory for names; it just sort of stuck in my mind."

"Damn your memory — and damn you! It's none of your business. She is a prisoner because of what she knows, just remember that."

"Yessir!" Red grinned. "What are you going to do with her, take her back to the Chesapeake and have her watched?"

Seth's frown deepened. "I don't know — no!"

"You can't be thinking of taking her to the island?"

"Why not? Travers is dead. Clinton told me it happened weeks ago. She was obviously on her way home to England."

"But the island is no place for a woman like that. Besides . . . " He looked at Seth. "What about Lilath?"

"What about Lilath? She will do as she is told or get out."

Red's eyes glinted as he thought of the beautiful quadroon girl who regarded Captain Thorn as her own special property. Seth had bought her from the Madam of a Charleston whore-house where she had been a slave. He brought her back to the island the pirates used as a base between raids and gave her her freedom. But she refused to leave his house and insisted on doing everything for him. She had jealously fought off all the other women who cast lustful eyes at *her* Captain, and she was generally accepted as Seth's woman. Lilath would not take kindly to the newcomer, that much was certain!

Seth saw Red's amused look and cursed. "It isn't what you are thinking. She is a nuisance, that's all. I can't let her go back to England, and I don't know what else to do with her. Take over command of the ship now; I am going below."

"Yessir!" Red grinned. "I'll tell the crew you are not to be disturbed, Captain."

"You will tell the crew nothing. Nothing! do you hear me? Especially about what I said the night I was drunk. If I hear one snigger about that I'll break your damned neck!"

Red's smile faded. "Sorry, Seth, I didn't realise she meant that much to you. I spoke out of turn. It won't happen again."

Seth glared at him. "She means nothing to me, damn you. Nothing!"

Red shook his head as his leader strode off angrily. The Captain was in a rare mood and no mistake. He hadn't seen him this way for months. Come to think of it, the last time was after he returned from that party at Clinton's house. He had snapped everyone's head off for days and drunk himself silly every night for a week. Then he had suddenly pulled himself out of it and the crew had heaved a sigh of relief. Red had wondered what happened that night, now he thought perhaps he knew.

★ ★ ★

Arabella looked up as the cabin door opened. She had been sitting with her eyes closed, trying to fight off her weariness. It was hours since she had been locked in. William had cried himself to sleep because he was hungry, and she herself was thirsty, but she could only find wine to drink.

She stood up as she saw Seth in the doorway, his dark eyes sweeping over her as if appraising her looks. Her face flushed with anger. How dare he treat her like this?

"I was beginning to wonder if you intended to let us die of thirst," she said, her voice as cold as the look in his eyes. "William has been crying for hours because he was hungry."

Seth blinked at her, thrown off balance by her attack. His emotions at seeing her on the *Susanah Yorke* had surprised him. He believed he had at last got her out of his system until he turned round and saw her standing there in her black gown. Then the desire to hold her in his arms rushed up in him like a great tide. The decision to bring her on board had been made in a rash moment and he had been half-regretting it ever since. What the hell was he going to do with her now?

"I am sorry, Mrs Travers, I had forgotten the child. I will have something suitable prepared for him."

"He is sleeping now: later, when he wakes, please."

She bit her lip. "I am rather thirsty myself and I could only find wine."

"Of course. I will have a meal sent into you."

He turned to leave.

"Seth — please don't go yet."

He stopped, hesitated and turned back to face her. "What else can I do for you, Mrs Travers?"

"Don't call me that!" Arabella was irritated. Why must he be so coldly polite? It would be better if he shouted at her. She could cope with his anger but not this icy indifference.

"I thought it was your name. You were Captain Travers' wife, were you not?"

"Yes." Arabella clenched her hands at her sides tensely. Was there no way she could reach him? "I was a convict on board his ship. When we reached

358

Virginia he bought my bond and then he married me."

Seth frowned. "I had heard such a rumour. I did not believe it, however. Why were you sent to Virginia as a convict, Arabella?"

His voice had softened slightly. Arabella hesitated, longing to tell him everything. But would he believe her, or would he think she was trying to play on his sympathy? She did not want his pity!

"It is not necessary for you to know that," she said, turning away so that he should not see she was close to tears. "I just wanted you to understand why I married Jethro."

"I presumed it was because you needed a father for Christopher Allingham's child," Seth's bitter words cut into her heart like a shaft of ice. "Wouldn't your English lord marry you when he discovered you were having another man's child? I realise now why you were in such a hurry to marry him."

Arabella whirled round, her eyes blazing with fury.

"Damn you, Seth Blackthorn! Why did you have to bring me on board your ship? Why did you not just let me go back to England? You've never forgiven me, have you? All right, so you weren't the first to make love to me, but I tried to tell you I was sorry. God! I wished I could turn back time and cut Christopher out of my life, but I couldn't. And your stupid pride wouldn't let you believe I loved you. You thought I would betray you!"

"Arabella . . . " Seth stared at her. God, but she was lovely! He remembered the night he had seen her at Clinton's party wearing that outrageous gown. He had wanted to kill her. It had taken every ounce of willpower he possessed to keep from breaking her beautiful neck. He had been forced to swallow his wrath and greet her and her husband politely, leaving the gathering the first moment he could. Since then he had managed to build up a barrier of hatred and scorn against her in his heart.

Arabella gasped as she saw the cold fury in his eyes; she backed away from him, shivering. "Don't come near me, Seth. If you try to touch me I'll fight you." She snatched up a wicked-looking knife from his desk. "I'll use this rather than let you touch me!"

Seth's mood of indecision left him in an instant, now he knew why he had brought her on board the *Fateful*. He still wanted her. All the drinking, fighting and whoring hadn't eased his hunger for her. There was only one way to do that. He wanted her and he was damned well going to have her whenever he felt like it! She was nothing but a whore and he was going to treat her like one!

He grabbed her wrist, twisting it cruelly until the knife dropped from her bloodless fingers, then he pulled her into his arms, grinding his lips on hers in a brutal kiss.

Arabella went for him like a wildcat,

clawing at his face, scratching and biting. She screamed as he picked her up bodily and slung her over his shoulder, beating at his back with her fists. He carried her to the bed and flung her down, grinning at her look of fury as he began to strip off his clothes. She gave an angry cry and tried to get up but he pushed her back, holding her carelessly with one hand.

"Lie still, Arabella," he muttered. "You asked for this and you are going to get it. You can have it easy or rough, please yourself."

Arabella lay back on the pillows as he began to unlace her bodice, stubbornly refusing to make it easy for him as he fumbled with the strings. She was breathing heavily, her sea-green eyes glittering angrily even as she admitted defeat. He could take her against her will no matter how hard she fought him, but her anger was even more for herself than for him. With a little shock of dismay she realised she was trembling, not from fear but with desire. Every part of her body ached to be touched by him. Only her pride would not let her admit how much she wanted him.

"I hate you," she said bitterly, making no attempt to stop him as he lifted her hips to pull off her petticoats.

Then she was naked, her eyes meeting his defiantly as he stood over her. He stared at her hungrily, letting his eyes devour the firm, full breasts, travelling down past the taut, flat belly to the fair, matted hair below. Groaning as the desire became a physical pain, he bent over her, kissing the creamy-gold throat, then her breasts, her navel.

Arabella gave a little cry of shock as his lips slid even lower, seeking the very essence of her. She could not believe what he was doing to her, nor begin to understand the wild ecstasy his darting tongue aroused in her. She had never experienced anything so shocking and yet so wholly exquisite in her life. She moaned softly as her senses reeled, sending her mad with delight. She was no longer able to make even a feeble pretence of fighting him. So that when at last he lowered his firm, lean body to hers, raising his hips slightly to thrust into her, she arched her back to meet him in a fever of desire. Her lips parted for his kiss, tasting the slightly aromatic flavour of herself.

It was even better than their first loving. Having his child had stretched her sufficiently for her to accommodate him without the pain she had experienced before. She jerked with little spasms of delight as they reached the climax of their loving together. Exhausted and panting, she lay looking at him. He reached out to touch her cheek, running his finger lightly down it to her slender throat.

"So you hate me, Bella," he murmured softly. "Well, that makes us even. I've hated you for a long time."

"Seth?" She opened her eyes wide in shock. He couldn't mean it surely! Not after what had just happened!

"Bella, my lovely, cheating, little bitch. I've never found another woman to ease my hunger for you — so we'll just agree to hate each other. You are mine just as much as the rest of the cargo we took from the *Susanah Yorke*, and I intend to keep you. You will be my own private whore for as long as I want you."

Arabella sat up, letting her mane of pale silk fall forward over her face so that he should not see the pain in her eyes.

"And when you don't want me anymore?"

He rolled away from her and began to dress.

"We will discuss that when it happens." He glanced at William who was still fast asleep. "I'll arrange some food for the child, and a meal for us." At Arabella's startled look, he laughed. "You didn't think I would be satisfied that easily, did you? I have been fasting for a long, long time, my sweet — and I intend to make up for it!"

10

THE ship lay at anchor in the sheltered bay, the palm-fringed beaches protected on two sides by long arms of rocks which made the narrow entrance difficult to navigate and almost impossible to spot from the open sea. It was this circumstance, discovered by accident, which had prompted the crew of the *Fateful* to choose this particular island as their haven, believing it safe from the British patrol ships which had done so much damage to the ranks of the buccaneers over the last fifty-odd years. Once, men like Henry Morgan had reigned supreme in these waters, men of several nationalities united in their fierce hatred of the Spanish, and using that hatred as an excuse to plunder the rich treasure ships. The war between Britain and France at the end of the last century had broken their ranks, and Britain's ever-growing naval power had almost succeeded in wiping them out.

Seth believed in his heart that if the *Fateful* continued to attack ships of different nations at random, her crew would eventually die at the rope's end. For himself he had almost had enough of the life, having amassed sufficient wealth for his future plans; and when the war broke out between America and Britain, he intended to offer his services to the Americans. Afterwards — well, afterwards could take care of itself. His immediate problems were more pressing.

Last night the *Fateful* had sailed into the bay, after dropping off the cargo of tobacco and the secret papers at a prearranged rendezvous. Lilath had been one of the first to come scrambling aboard. But the eager light in her eyes as she ran barefoot across the deck to meet Seth died as she saw Arabella, to be replaced by a yellow flare of pure hatred.

"Who is she?" she hissed.

"This is Bella: she is my woman," he said, meeting her furious gaze steadily.

"Lilath your woman! White woman no good for you. She bad, bad woman. Bring evil to you, my Captain. I see fire all round you." Lilath rolled her eyes expressively. "You hurting bad. It is this woman who brings the fire."

Seth laughed, putting his arm around her waist and swinging her off her feet to kiss her soundly. "You are trying to frighten me, Lilath. If you are very good I might keep you, too. Two women must be better than one."

He was conscious of Arabella's cold fury as she stood behind him, watching with her eyes narrowed. He kissed Lilath again, deliberately taunting Arabella, knowing that she would be humiliated and hurt. He wondered why she alone could rouse such passion in him. It was knowing she had so much power over him that made him cruel. He wanted to make her suffer as he had suffered, to let her feel the sting of naked jealousy. But most of all he wanted to possess her utterly. He thought that he would never have enough of her.

He let Lilath go suddenly. "You will leave my house tonight," he whispered in her ear as he released her. "Find yourself another man, Lilath."

Lilath stared at him, her beautiful, coffee-coloured face a mask of rage and pain. Her tawny eyes flashed angrily. "Batard!" she spat at him; using the language of the man who had sired her and then sold her to the Madam of a Charleston whorehouse at the tender age of twelve. "Cochon!"

Seth grinned as she lashed out at him with her long nails, neatly avoiding their wicked slash. She stared at him with a mixture of hatred and love in her yellow eyes. Then she gave a little sob, turned and fled, disappearing over the side of the ship as she dived into the calm blue waters of the bay.

When Seth arrived at the small wooden house he used on his visits to the island, Lilath's few possessions had gone. He felt no regret for the harsh way he had used her: Lilath understood nothing else. If he had been gentle with her she would have laughed in his face and disobeyed him. He had realised his mistake soon after he brought her to the island. He had bought her on impulse, feeling sorry for the lovely girl who was still only seventeen and who had already spent five years as the slave of the old Madam, forced to give her body to any man who could pay. Afterwards she had begged him to take her with him, and he had been foolish enough to agree. She was a passionate bedmate, but she left him cold and empty when their wild mating was over. Only one woman made him feel really good, and that woman was not Lilath.

His hunger for Arabella had not abated on the voyage to the island. He had taken her again and again, sometimes coming close to rape in his brutal treatment of her; but always it ended with tender kisses and loving that almost drained his very soul. It seemed that he died in her arms, only to have his desire rekindled the moment she whispered his name. And however harshly he treated her, however much he hurt her, she won. God, how he loved her!

No, he hated her! She was a wanton, faithless bitch. His mind told him to remember it while his heart and body denied it. She was both Heaven and Hell to him. It did not matter. Love her or hate her, he could not live without her. He never wanted to go back to the barren waste which had held him prisoner from the moment he sent her out of his life. She was his. His! No matter how much they hurt each other, she was his woman. He would never let her go.

Lilath remained a problem, however. She had disappeared from the compound and no one had seen her that morning. But she was a wildcat and Seth knew she would be waiting for her chance to be revenged on him, or Arabella.

He would have to watch out for her or she might stick a knife in his back, or more likely Arabella's. His fear was wholly for the woman he loved. He could take care of himself, but could Arabella?

★ ★ ★

The two women faced each other across the clear waters of the shallow stream. Arabella was already immersed in the sun-warmed water, having taken off all her clothes to indulge in the pleasure of a private swim. She had slipped away from the cluster of wooden houses in the pirates' compound to a secluded spot several minutes' walk away, wanting the chance to bathe and wash her hair. All the water on the island had to be fetched from one of the plentiful streams, and it had seemed so much simpler to come here alone rather than carry the water up to the house. And the stream nearest to the encampment was in constant use. She knew she was safe enough from the other pirates, none of whom would have dared to follow her, let alone lay a finger on Captain Thorn's woman; but Seth had warned her that Lilath might try to attack her. She had laughed at him then, growing more certain that Lilath would stay away from her as the days passed. But now she was not quite so sure. The quadroon girl must have been watching her and waiting for the right moment.

Arabella waded to the shore and began to put on her clothes unhurriedly, knowing that the other woman was staring at her naked body. Let her look, Arabella thought, uncaring of the jealousy in those yellow eyes. She turned to meet the vicious hatred in Lilath's stare just as the quadroon girl sprang at her.

Taken by surprise, Arabella went down under the tigerish attack; but then she began to fight back. The two of them rolled over and over on the ground, and into the shallows of the stream.

Lilath was pulling at Arabella's long hair, screaming like a banshee. Now she screamed even louder as she suddenly found herself dislodged and pinioned beneath Arabella's knees. Her screams stopped abruptly as Arabella forced her head beneath the water and held it there. She gasped and struggled wildly for a while, then went limp. Moments later she found herself dragged on the bank, opening her eyes to see Arabella bending over her.

"Had enough?" Arabella asked. "I've met your kind before — so just remember I can use a knife if I have to."

Lilath choked and spat water, her chest heaving as she fought to recover her breath. "I will kill you," she gasped. "You stole my Captain. I will kill you."

Arabella smiled. "He was mine long before he knew you," she said. "I just took him back, that's all. Admit defeat, Lilath."

"Never!" Lilath suddenly spat in Arabella's face. "He my Captain before you came; he be mine again when you dead!"

Arabella wiped the spittle from her face. She gave the other girl a wry smile. Who would have believed that she, Arabella Pennington, would be prepared to fight for the love of a man she had once considered so far beneath her that a marriage was out of the question? How much she had changed since those far-off days of innocence.

"You will just have to try harder next time, won't you?" she said, then turned and walked away, leaving the quadroon girl staring after her with a look of pure hatred.

"I will kill you, white woman," Lilath whispered. "You and the baby with the dark eyes. Then my Captain be free of you."

Seth was down at the beach supervising the loading of stores for their next voyage when he saw the smoke rising from the direction of the compound. He shouted to his companions, beginning to run across the sand towards the cluster of wooden buildings. With the stiff breeze blowing over the island today the whole lot could catch light in a moment. And Arabella was there somewhere!

As he reached the compound he saw that it was his own house which was on fire, the flames already licking round the wooden balcony. Arabella came rushing to meet him, her hair flying in the wind. She clutched at him wildly, her eyes dark with fear.

"William is in there!" she cried. "I left him sleeping while I went to fetch water. When I came back the house was on fire. I can't get in, Seth. I can't get in!"

Seth stared at the house, hesitating.

It was an inferno. He doubted whether he could reach the boy himself.

Arabella beat at his chests with her fists, losing all control in her terror for her son. "Don't let him die," she begged, sobbing. "Don't let your own son die, Seth!"

Seth stared at her, then he began to run towards the house.

The pirates had already formed a chain with buckets of water to douse the flames. Seth grabbed one of the buckets, ripping off his shirt and soaking it in the water, then he went inside. The smoke was so thick that it penetrated the damp material he held pressed over his nose and mouth. But by some miracle the staircase had not yet caught fire.

He ran up the wooden steps, taking them two at a time and crashing through the door of William's room. The heat inside was intense and one wall was a solid mass of flame, but he saw the child huddled under a pile of blankets, whimpering. Seth seized

William, and wrapping him completely in the blankets, he started back for the stairs. At the top he paused seeing that the bottom three stairs were engulfed in flames. He hesitated for a second, but there was no other way out. Holding William tightly against his chest with one arm, he covered his own face as best he could and charged through the flames.

He could feel the heat licking at his naked arms and back, and the pain was sharp, but then he was out in the fresh air, choking out the foul smoke in his lungs. He threw William to Red, who was pacing up and down outside the mass of flames like a caged animal, frustrated by his inability to help; then he flung himself down on the ground rolling in the sandy earth to extinguish the burning cloth which had been his breeches.

Arabella had taken the screaming child from Red, running her hands over him in a fever of anxiety until she found he was unharmed. Then she gave him into the arms of one of the other women and went to Seth, who was lying face downwards on the ground. She gasped as she saw his smoke-blackened skin and the burnt rags clinging to his muscled thighs. She knelt beside him on the sandy earth, her hands hovering over him but not daring to touch for fear of hurting him.

"Oh, Seth, my darling, my love," she wept. "Oh God, you are hurt, you are hurt. Oh, Seth, Seth, don't die!"

The tears were pouring down her cheeks as Seth rolled over and looked at her, managing a grin despite his pain. "I am not about to die, Bella," he said. "You won't get rid of me that easily."

"Oh, Seth . . . " Arabella choked back her tears, feeling slightly hysterical.

She watched as he struggled to his feet, wincing at the effort. She sat back on her heels, wanting to help him but afraid to move.

Seth looked at the burns on the back

of his hands and his arms, realising that he had been lucky. The fire had merely licked at him as he burst through, the wounds were not deep. His flesh was already smarting like hell, but he knew he was fortunate to be alive. It had been an insane thing to do, but no power on earth could have held him back once he knew William was his son. *His son*! He looked for the boy as Red came up to him, his face grim.

"It was Lilath," he said. "One of the men saw her running away. She knew you were at the beach, and she must have thought Arabella was still inside."

"The bitch! I never should have brought her here. Tell the men I want her found."

"It is already done. Rotten Willie caught her."

"Thank God for that! She'll have to be sent away. I cannot risk this happening again . . . "

Red looked uncomfortable. "You had better come up to my house. The fire is under control now, and those burns need some attention."

Seth stared at him suspiciously, recognising that look of old. "What are you hiding, Red?"

Red sighed, realising his leader would be angry. "Rotten Willie got her; you know what he is. She's dead, Seth. She pulled a knife on him and he killed her."

Seth closed his eyes for a moment, anger and hopelessness washing over him at the wanton waste of life. "The poor, silly bitch," he said. "Why did she do it?"

Red shrugged. "I knew something like this would happen; thank God it was no worse. Come on now, let me help you."

Seth nodded wearily, the first numbness was wearing off now and the pain had started in earnest. He glanced at Arabella who was still weeping silently as she tried to comfort William: his son. Seth held out his hand to her.

"Will you come with me?" he asked, his voice very gentle. "Please."

Arabella nodded, moving to his side. They looked at each other, neither of them needing words. They both knew that something had changed between them.

"Yes, Seth," she whispered.

★ ★ ★

The gentle lapping of the water against the ship's sides was all that broke the silence as Arabella turned in her lover's arms. She reached out in the darkness, tracing the beloved features of his face with her fingers.

"Are you awake?" she whispered.

His arms tightened around her slender waist. "Will you never be satisfied, wench?" he asked.

She laughed huskily, pressing her lips against his throat. "No, never. It has been a lifetime since you were well enough to . . . " She broke off as he suddenly rolled her beneath him, imprisoning her with his hard, lean body. She ran her hand over his back lightly, feeling the partially-healed blisters rough to her touch. She experienced a rush of love for him remembering how the scars had been won. "Be careful, my love, don't hurt yourself."

For answer he brought his mouth down to hers, brushing her lips with a tenderness that set her tingling with love and desire.

"Oh, Seth," she breathed. "I love you so much. You will never know how much."

"Show me," he demanded, catching her bottom lip between his strong teeth and nibbling it gently. "Show me how much you love me, Bella."

Arabella obliged very willingly, her lips kissing and tasting every part of his body, licking the pearls of sweat from his skin. He shuddered as she moved unerringly to that part of him where he most wanted to feel her tantalising kisses. He gasped as the exquisite pleasure throbbed through him, half-crazed by the sensuous movements of her mouth. Unable to bear the sweet agony longer, he pressed her back on the bed, taking her passionately, holding her slim body against him even when his passion was spent, as though he could not bear to part from her ever again.

Later, he said: "Why did you not tell me William was mine?" He rolled on his back, still holding her to him so that she lay pressed against him.

Arabella caressed his dark hair. "I wanted you to love me, not just my son. Besides, I thought you must guess it as soon as you saw his eyes. He has your eyes, Seth."

"I hoped — sometimes I was almost sure, but you said nothing. You did not deny it when I said he was Allingham's child."

Arabella sighed and tried to move away but he would not let her go. "I did not think you would believe me. You did not believe me that night you came back to Pennington Towers. I was marrying Lord Greenvale for your sake, Seth, even though that was not the reason I first accepted his offer." She felt him tense and her fingers reached into his hair, jerking it viciously. "Listen to me, damn you! Don't freeze me out again!"

He relaxed slightly, still holding her. "I am listening."

"I always loved you, Seth, the trouble was I did not know it at first. I thought you were beneath me. I thought it would shame me to marry a farmer's son — Are you angry?"

He shook his head in the darkness. "No, I understood how you felt. I felt it myself, but I couldn't stop loving you."

"I lied to you when I said I went to Christopher because Rose told me you were the father of her child; I was afraid you would not believe me if I told you the truth."

"And that was?" His voice was ice cold.

"He is evil, Seth, like a serpent that worms its way into your bed and stings you to death. He heard us talking in my father's study that night, and he threatened to tell my father unless I went to his room." Seth was silent for a moment, then: "Go on — that isn't the whole of it, Bella. I know you are holding something back."

"I couldn't sleep all that night. In the morning I rode down to the farm: I was going to run away with you but you had gone. Allingham threatened me again that evening, and I did not know what to do. I was afraid that if my father learned the truth he would have you arrested and your parents turned out of their home . . . "

"So you went to his room: did he rape you?"

"No." Arabella's voice shook as she tried to keep calm. "I hated him, Seth, but he was a skilful lover — he made me respond to him. He wanted my complete surrender . . . " She paused but Seth did not speak so she went on: "He left me after my father's death without even a message of regret. I was nothing but a broken toy to be discarded at will. By this time I believed you had betrayed me as well. I thought I hated all men and I was determined to take all I could from them — that's why I said I would marry Lord Greenvale. But everything changed when you made love to me that afternoon, then . . . "

"Then?" Seth's voice was harsh with pain.

"And then I knew that no other man would ever make me feel quite like that, because you were the only man I would ever love. I cannot help my nature, Seth, or pretend I have not known pleasure in another man's arms, but afterwards I always felt empty. At first I couldn't bear Jethro to touch me, then it got better but it meant nothing to me. Afterwards I would go to William's room and weep because I knew how much I had lost. You must understand what I mean — I haven't exactly been the only woman in your life, have I?"

"No." Seth's arms tightened about her suddenly. "You cannot help your nature, Bella, any more than I can help mine. I shall always hate the thought of another man ever having touched you."

"I know." The tears slid silently down her cheeks and fell on to his face. "Please forgive me, Seth. Please!"

"Don't cry, my darling. I have forgiven you. You say you weren't raped by Allingham, but I think you were: it was a rape of your senses, a rape of your innocence and your right to choose, perhaps even more cruel in its way than a physical rape." He kissed her throat, running his hands over her satin skin, pressing her hard against him as though he would absorb her into his own flesh. "I love you, that's enough. It has to be. I can't live without you ever again."

Arabella laid her head against his chest. "I love you, only you."

"I know." He gently stroked her hair. "Why were you a convict, Bella, will you tell me now?"

"I — I tried to kill Richard. He betrayed you to the Revenue men, Seth. He told me so." She would not tell him what else Richard had done: he had been hurt enough, and she never wanted to cause him pain again. "He locked me in my room until after you were taken. I nearly went out of my mind when I thought you were dead."

"Oh, Bella." Seth held her even closer. "My beautiful, crazy Bella! Will you marry me?"

"Why — because you want your son?"

Seth chuckled. "You suspicious wench! No, because I intend to make certain no other man ever gets his hands on you again. Well, will you marry a pirate?"

Arabella laughed huskily in the darkness. "Yes, oh, yes, Seth."

"Why are you laughing?"

Arabella wound her arms around his

neck. "You must remind me to tell you my family history one day," she whispered against his mouth as she began to kiss him lingeringly.

"But not just now . . . "

THE END

WITH SOMEBODY ELSE
Theresa Charles

Rosamond sets off for Cornwall with Hugo to meet his family, blissfully unaware of the shocks in store for her.

A SUMMER FOR STRANGERS
Claire Hamilton

Because she had lost her job, her flat and she had no money, Tabitha agreed to pose as Adam's future wife although she believed the scheme to be deceitful and cruel.

VILLA OF SINGING WATER
Angela Petron

The disquieting incidents that occurred at the Vatican and the Colosseum did not trouble Jan at first, but then they became increasingly unpleasant and alarming.

DOCTOR NAPIER'S NURSE
Pauline Ash

When cousins Midge and Derry are entered as probationer nurses on the same day but at different hospitals they agree to exchange identities.

A GIRL LIKE JULIE
Louise Ellis

Caroline absolutely adored Hugh Barrington, but then Julie Crane came into their lives. Julie was the kind of girl who attracts men without even trying.

COUNTRY DOCTOR
Paula Lindsay

When Evan Richmond bought a practice in a remote country village he did not realise that a casual encounter would lead to the loss of his heart.

ENCORE
Helga Moray

Craig and Janet realise that their true happiness lies with each other, but it is only under traumatic circumstances that they can be reunited.

NICOLETTE
Ivy Preston

When Grant Alston came back into her life, Nicolette was faced with a dilemma. Should she follow the path of duty or the path of love?

THE GOLDEN PUMA
Margaret Way

Catherine's time was spent looking after her father's Queensland farm. But what life was there without David, who wasn't interested in her?